Montana
★ MAVERICKS

Welcome to Montana—the home of bold men
and daring women, where more than fifty tales
of passion, adventure and intrigue unfold
beneath the Big Sky. Don't miss a single one!

Montana ★ MAVERICKS

MYRNA MACKENZIE

Just Pretending

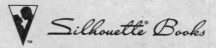

Silhouette Books

Published by Silhouette Books

America's Publisher of Contemporary Romance

Special thanks and acknowledgment to Myrna Mackenzie
for her contribution to the Montana Mavericks series.

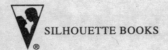

SILHOUETTE BOOKS

Recycling programs
for this product may
not exist in your area.

ISBN-13: 978-0-373-31057-9

JUST PRETENDING

Copyright © 2000 by Harlequin Books S.A.

Visit Silhouette Books at www.eHarlequin.com

Printed in U.S.A.

MYRNA MACKENZIE

is a winner of the Holt Medallion honoring outstanding fiction and a finalist for numerous other awards including an Orange Rose, a National Readers' Choice Award, a *Romantic Times BOOKreviews* Reviewer's Choice and Wis RWA's Write Touch. She believes that humor, love and hope are three of the best medicines in the world and tries to make sure that her books reflect that belief.

Born in a small town in Southern Missouri, Myrna grew up in the Chicago area, married her high-school sweetheart and has two teenage sons. Her hobbies include dreaming of warmer climes during the cold northern winters, pretending the dust in her house doesn't exist, taking long walks and traveling. Readers can write to Myrna at P.O. Box 225, LaGrange, IL 60525, or they may visit her online at www.myrnamackenzie.com.

One

The town of Whitehorn, Montana, didn't look as though it had just been kicked in the teeth, David Hannon thought as he pushed through the outer doors of the police station. The July sky was blue, the sun was out, the mountains in the background were spectacular, and the town appeared to be every man's vision of the perfect place to settle down. But, of course, if everything in his hometown had been perfect lately, he wouldn't be here. At least not on a search for the truth.

David moved beyond the sunlight and into the station. He removed his dark sunglasses, smiled down at the middle-aged woman sitting behind the desk and told her who he was and who he wanted to see. She scribbled his message down on a scrap of paper and excused herself.

"Hey, Hannon, it's been forever. Good to see you," a booming voice called, snagging his attention as David walked further into the room and grinned at the deputy sheriff heading his way. "But if you wanted to catch any of those weddings your family's been staging lately, you're too late. Of course, the way your clan has been falling, there might be something Cupid's slipped into the water supply. Better watch out. You could be next. Just another smooth bachelor fallen facedown in the wedding cake."

David shook his head, still grinning as he reached out to shake his old friend's hand. There *had* been a couple of unexpected weddings in his family in the past few months. But that wasn't why he had returned.

"Reed, it's great to see you, too. And you're right. I only wish I could have made it here in time for both Frannie's and Cleo's weddings, but I couldn't get away at the time." It was the truth. It had nearly killed him that he hadn't been able to get here in time to see the sister and cousin he was crazy about each take their turn walking down the aisle.

"So, you missed the weddings and now you're here for…"

"To see my home and family, kiss the brides, congratulate the grooms on their good fortune, say hi to all my old buddies," he said. "Do a little nosing around while I'm here."

"Thought so," the man said. "Can't blame you. I'd be doing the same, if it were me, considering all the things that have been going on."

Another deputy showed up and slapped David on the back. "David, it's good to see that pretty face of yours. You don't come around nearly enough. Means less women fainting at your feet, more dates for me, but still we've all missed you, bud. I couldn't help but hear what you said. That nosing around you're talking about have anything to do with those bodies that were found at the future resort/casino site out on Kincaid land?"

David tilted his head, reluctant to say too much until he knew which way the clouds were rolling in. "I thought I'd see if I could help out."

"In an official capacity? FBI send you to assist?"

More like they hadn't stopped him. His superior had known where David was going when he requested a leave of absence and he also knew what was going on here in Whitehorn, but David was overdue for some time off. Still, it was a mark of Phil's confidence in his professionalism that the man had okayed the leave without question. "Don't get in too deep, Hannon, or I'll have to call you back," was his only comment. David didn't plan to give Phil any reason to do that, but he fully intended to get at the truth of what had happened here in his hometown.

"Yeah, are you here as Special Agent Hannon or simply as David Hannon, one of Whitehorn's favorite wandering sons?" another man asked with a chuckle.

"We'll see," David answered with a shrug and a grin. "Who's the chief investigating officer on this one?" A lot would depend on how open-minded and cooperative the officer was.

The men exchanged a few sidelong glances. "That would be Detective Neal. Over there," one man said.

David turned and looked toward the back of the room where his old friend had pointed and met with a sea-green-eyed stare and a pair of raised delicate blond brows. She was tall, slender, very crisp, her white blouse a sharp contrast to her black pantsuit. Her outfit and her demeanor said she was no-nonsense, just as her position required her to be. Nothing unusual about that. David had worked with plenty of female special agents, trusted his back to more than a few. Some of them had been colleagues, some friends, some more. None of them had ever made him think of hot nights and tangled sheets and drinking champagne from a woman's lips. Until this second, that is. This lady detective was definitely a very special case, and she was frowning at him right now. She made one last comment to the person she'd been conversing with and started walking his way.

"Detective Neal?" David asked the man standing next to him.

"Very definitely, Hannon. Have a care. Gretchen's relatively new to the area, but she's one of the best. Worked the streets of Miami for a while. She's knowledgeable, she's fair and caring, but she's tough. You may be able to charm most women with a single crook of your finger, but Gretchen takes her work very seriously and if you don't do the same, she bites."

The man's words were teasing, but David could hear the respect in his friend's voice.

"I wouldn't imagine the sheriff would give his biggest case to someone who didn't know how to do the job. Rafe's too smart for that," he agreed.

"She know who and what you are?" the man asked.

"Could be. Or maybe not. Catch you later," David said quietly as he strode toward Detective Neal.

He didn't know what the lady knew about him other than that he'd sent a note asking to see her, and those killer green eyes told him nothing. She moved across the room with purpose and efficiency, studying him as she advanced.

"Mr. Hannon?" she asked, looking down at the note the officer at the desk had taken to her. She stepped up beside David and he noted that in spite of his six-foot-one-inch frame, she didn't have to look up very far to stare into his eyes. "You must be related to Frannie, then?"   "My sister," he agreed.

"Frannie was one of the first people I met when I arrived here," the lady said with a carefully polite smile. "She made a stranger feel welcome. But you didn't come here to talk about your family. You're here on police business, I'm told. You know something of one of my cases? You have information you'd like to provide to the authorities, perhaps, Mr. Hannon?"

Her voice was the cool smoky kind that could make a man think about bed when he should be thinking about business. Her thick, honeyed hair moved as she spoke, brushing her jawline. David had an undeniable itch to reach out and sample the silky texture of the tempting shimmery stuff. Like a curious child, he mused. Or a man in the mood to get his face slapped. He tilted his lips up in a bemused grin.

"I'm here on a matter of public concern, Detective Neal," he said, schooling his thoughts to the matter at hand. "You're handling the Raven Hunter murder and the death of Peter Cook. I understand that both bodies were found on the site of the future resort/casino being built in the area and that Peter Cook was one of the employees on the site. I'm here to look into those cases."

She raised one brow. "What reason would you have for doing that, Mr. Hannon?" she asked, that boudoir voice quiet but firm.

"David," he said simply. "Special agent. FBI," he added, removing his credentials from the pocket of his sports jacket and flashing them. "I have reason to believe I could be of service here."

"I see."

He doubted that very much, but he could see something. Those beautiful green eyes had narrowed. He'd at least gotten her complete attention.

"I haven't heard anything from the Bureau indicating that you were on your way, Mr. Hannon," she said, ignoring his suggestion that she call him by his first name. "You're telling me you've been assigned to my case for some reason?"

"I don't recall putting it that way."

"Just what way would you put it, then? If you're not here officially, why would you offer your services?"

"This is my home. I have an interest."

"And Jeremiah Kincaid, the chief suspect in the Raven Hunter murder, was your uncle."

David nodded his agreement. "We weren't close."

The lady took a deep breath. "There was animosity between you?"

The slight look of hope in her eyes had David smiling. "Nice try, Detective, but no, I wouldn't say that. I didn't really know Jeremiah well. He didn't take much interest in his sisters' offspring. The man had...other interests." The wary look that crossed the lady's face told David that she knew exactly what he meant and that she was wondering if the family traits were passed down through the male bloodlines. His uncle had been an infamous womanizer.

As for David, he'd been blessed with more than his share of female companionship, and he hadn't failed to notice that while Gretchen Neal did her best to shelve her femininity during working hours, she couldn't hide that rose-and-cream complexion of hers. But just because he'd noticed the lady's skin, that didn't mean he was anything like his disreputable uncle.

David held out his hands in a gesture of surrender, but he arched one brow in obvious challenge.

"Look, Detective, I'll be honest. I'm interested in this case because this is my hometown. It's no secret that the people on the Laughing Horse Reservation have wanted to build this casino and resort for a while and that it will bring them much needed revenue. It's also no secret that this deal has been made possible only because the people from the rez and a few private investors have joined forces to cross reservation lines and build some badly needed bridges between the town and the reservation. Like everyone else here, I want that to succeed. Finding bodies on the affected land has put a halt to that construction and those bridges for now, so, yes, I have an interest in that sense. But I'm also interested because all these 'discoveries,' these bodies, seem to have upset my aunt Celeste tremendously. Jeremiah was her brother, Raven was the father of her niece, Summer, and this brings back memories of her sister Blanche's death, as well. She's naturally upset, so much so that she isn't sleeping. She isn't eating right, I'm told. If I can help in any way, assist with the case and help move things more quickly, I'd want to do that."

"There's no reason for you to get involved. This is a homicide. Not an FBI matter. Raven Hunter's remains weren't found on the reservation, and the Whitehorn force is an excellent one. We're capable of handling this alone." Gretchen Neal's tone and her demeanor projected absolute calm. She was good, but not good enough to hide that trace element of annoyance in her eyes. She was in charge here and she didn't like the implication that she needed outside help to do her job.

"I'm not implying that you're not capable, Detective," David said, keeping his voice cool and soothing. "That doesn't mean that this department, just like any other law enforcement agency, couldn't use a little assistance when it's offered gratis. You can't tell me that this special arrangement doesn't follow standard procedure, because Whitehorn has never really been known for doing that. You've got Rafe, a county sheriff, in charge of officers in the town and deputy sheriffs out into the rest of the county. Those jobs have always overlapped, and territories have been crossed when it was necessary to keep the citizens of the area safe. It's a maverick setup that makes Whitehorn special—and effective. Why not take it a step farther and get a little help from another agency, as well?"

The smallest of smiles lifted her lips and David had the feeling that he'd been given an unexpected gift. Her smile transformed her face, making her eyes light up. He had an urge to take a step closer. He squelched it, sure that this lady who was fighting so hard to keep him out of her investigation definitely wouldn't want him in her personal space.

"You like to argue, don't you, Mr. Hannon?" she asked with a touch of laughter in her voice. "Well, you're right, I can't debate the procedural issue, but that doesn't mean it's a good idea to take on volunteer officers. We've had plenty of work trying to keep the site uncontaminated. People seem to want to flock to a murder scene for some reason. I'm sorry, but in my book, you'd be another warm body wandering over the site."

She stood her ground, her green gaze apologetic but immovable. David had to give Gretchen Neal credit. She wasn't going to let just anyone waltz in here and start calling the shots. He could see why Rafe Rawlings had put her in charge.

He raised one brow. "You make a good point there, Detective Neal, but I can assure you that won't be a problem. In my line of work, dead bodies show up more often than I care to remember." As always, David did his best not to think back on those scenes. Moving on was the only way to get past the memories and deal with the job effectively. He didn't like sloppy work any more than Gretchen Neal did.

"Ms. Neal," he continued. "I assure you I'll keep my warm body out of the way as much as possible. I'm here to help, not to hinder." His voice swooped low on those last words, almost the way a man would speak to a lover, and the lady blinked. She raised her chin higher, the slightest touch of rose in her cheeks just about the only hint that she was anything other than calm. He understood her consternation. He'd been a loner for most of his life and he knew all about that need to hold everything close, that unwillingness to give up even one thread of control to anyone.

For one second, one very brief second when she looked up at him, David could have sworn that the look in Gretchen Neal's eyes spoke of vulnerability. Immediately the shades came down on her soul.

"I'm sure you mean well, but I—that is, I really don't know you, Mr. Hannon, so I can't very well take your word on that, can I? Would you take me on without question if the circumstances were reversed?"

A low chuckle sounded behind her and David was

glad for the interruption. She made a good point, an excellent point, but he wasn't sure just how he would have answered. Gretchen Neal was an eyeful and an armful—and a good cop, according to her co-workers and his own gut instinct. David had the feeling she'd be a hard lady to turn away from.

"Easy, Gretch," Rafe Rawlings, sheriff and owner of the low chuckle said. "I know this guy. He's clean. How've you been, David?"

"Busy," David said with a smile as he shook hands with the sheriff. "But probably not as busy as you appear to have been lately."

Rafe shrugged. "I hear you're going to give us a hand. In an unofficial capacity, that is. Just heard from Phil Baker."

"In an unofficial way," David agreed.

"Rafe, have you considered the problems? This case is personal for Mr. Hannon," Gretchen said.

Rafe held up one hand. "You know almost everyone in town, Gretchen, and so do I. All our cases are personal."

"They're not family."

"David's a pro. One of the best and brightest. He'll handle it."

She opened her mouth, then shut it again, but her eyes were worried when she hazarded a glance at David. Clearly she wouldn't take her argument to the next step, blatantly questioning his professionalism, but she still didn't like the situation.

"It's a good move, Gretchen," Rafe said quietly. "David's lived here all his life. I know him. He cares what happens here. He'll make a good partner. You lead. He'll assist. Tomorrow will be soon enough to start. You're a pro, too, Gretch. Get over your objections by the morning. That's an order."

She sighed and nodded slightly. "You're the sheriff, Sheriff."

Rafe smiled, his eyes crinkling at the corners as he said goodbye and strolled away.

"Partners?" she whispered, her consternation evident.

David wanted to smile at the break in her voice, but he restrained himself. This lady didn't want him around at all, and he'd already won the battle. No point in aggravating the good detective.

"Get to know me, Neal, before you decide I'm the enemy. I'm interested in the truth," he said quietly. "And I intend to follow this through to the end no matter what that truth may turn out to be."

He also intended to discover another truth if he could, David thought as he bid her good-day. What was it about Gretchen Neal's soft green eyes that made him want to step in close and risk her bite? Just once before this case was closed, he hoped he'd get the chance to find out.

She'd argued too hard, Gretchen thought when David Hannon walked away, and she knew the reason. It wasn't because of his personal connection to the case, although she'd been right to question it and Rafe had been right to set her straight. It wasn't even because of the implication that she could use help from an outside agency, although her pride made her like to think that she could close this case alone. It did have something to do with the fact that this man was clearly going to be difficult to work with. He was going to want to lead.

She could tell that already. Even more than that, though, her resistance was because of her reaction the first moment she'd turned and seen David Hannon. There was something about that dark sweep of hair, those intense emerald eyes, that made a person feel as if he knew what sensual dreams flitted through her thoughts when she lay sleeping and open and vulnerable. He had a strong jaw and a mouth that was a slash of sinful temptation. He looked like a man who drank a lot of champagne out of a lot of women's slippers—and liked it.

Her breath had caught in her throat in a completely unprofessional way. It wasn't that she was unused to men giving her those speculative looks. She spent a lot of time with men. Most of her time, in fact, and she liked men. She liked dating, but she kept work and play very separate. She never got involved with other law enforcement officers. She never got involved with *anyone* too deeply and what's more, she didn't like feeling and doing things that just weren't smart. Having a physical reaction to David Hannon was plain stupid and unacceptable. Especially if she was going to work with him in close quarters.

And she was, it seemed, because when she arrived at the station the next morning David was there before her. When she walked up to her desk and found him lounging in her chair, studying a file, his tall, dark good looks hit her like an express train at full throttle. The man was smooth, James Bond smooth, with that wicked half smile and those deep knowing eyes that had, no doubt, convinced a good number of women that virginity was a very bad thing to hang on to. She'd just bet he knew how to use that face, that body and that convincing, seductive way of talking to get whatever he wanted, just as he had yesterday. Good thing she was a pro, Gretchen thought. She'd gotten past the wallop her first glance of David Hannon had given her and now she was back in charge. Of herself and this case. And she would remain that way.

"Ready to take me on?" he asked sweetly.

She smiled back at him just as sweetly. "I'm always ready and able to handle anything."

He raised one brow and grinned knowingly. Gretchen felt her heart trip over a speed bump too quickly, but she ignored the feeling.

"Let's get started, Mr. Hannon."

"David."

"David," she reluctantly agreed.

He waited, a patient smile on his lips.

"All right, okay, yes, I'm Gretchen," she finally said, reaching for the folder. "Shall we go…David?"

"Thought you'd never ask." He stood, looking down at her, and for one swift second she wished he were a little less tall, a little less broad-shouldered and polished. Maybe then she could think of him as just another cop of sorts. Must be the way he wore those sports jackets so elegantly or the fact that his white shirt looked good against his tanned skin.

"I'll fill you in as we drive," she managed to say, leading him out the door of the station to her plain white unmarked car. For one second, he headed for the driver's side, then paused, a sheepish smile on his face as she stopped dead in her tracks.

"Sorry, Gretchen."

"You're used to being in charge." Her words were resigned.

He shrugged, an admission of the truth. "I'm sure I'll get used to being second in command in time."

The last thing David Hannon was, was anyone's assistant. He was a man who knew how to lead and who liked to lead, and he was being gracious now by not pointing that out.

Gretchen sighed. "We'll both get used to it, David. Orders are orders."

As they cruised down the short streets of Whitehorn and out into the rolling, rugged country beyond, David studied Gretchen's profile. She was soft, fresh, a green-eyed beauty clad in another pristine pantsuit of stark navy. The dark suit and white blouse offset the golden glow of her hair, which feathered over her collar. Gretchen Neal might be a hard-edged detective, but she was packaged in the softness of a very womanly body. A delicious contrast.

She intrigued, and he was used to women intriguing. He'd grown up in Whitehorn, surrounded by his father and a number of females. His aunt, his mother, his sister and all those female cousins. Asthma had made him sickly, a victim of his condition, as a boy, and he'd grown used to a life surrounded by attentive, caring women. A life without close friends his age, it was true. He hadn't been able to do most of the things other kids had done. Still, he'd learned a lot about women in those years and he'd learned still more as he'd grown up and grown healthy. Women fascinated him and he'd enjoyed sampling more than his share. Gretchen was different, though. He could see that right from the start. Her shell was hard, as it had to be, but the core of her... well, that part of her fascinated him immensely. He very definitely wondered what exactly lay under that keep-your-distance armor of hers.

"You grew up in Miami?" he asked, his voice low and coaxing.

Her hands tightened on the wheel. "I grew up everywhere for a while. An army brat, but yes, we landed in Miami when I was ten."

"How'd you end up here?"

She turned for just a second to look at him and she shrugged, a small smile on her face.

"Trying to soften me up, David?"

He smiled as she turned back to the road. "Maybe. Mostly I'm just interested in knowing who you are. It's important for partners to know something of each other, don't you think? I'm responsible for your life from here on out. You're responsible for mine."

She glanced his way again, a dawning respect in the look she gave him. "You're right. It's very important to know whose hands you're placing your life in. I know I came on a bit strong yesterday, but I felt it was necessary, David."

"I never doubted your methods, your motives or your abilities, lady," he said seriously, truthfully. "Rafe chose you."

"And you. I'm sure you *are* good at what you do."

He tilted his head at her somewhat hesitant compliment. "How'd you end up in Whitehorn, Gretchen? This is a long way from the mean streets of Miami."

She smiled broadly for the first time, tilting her head up with pleasure, her smile sliding into her eyes to light them up like pale green flames, and David felt a zip of heated sensation shoot straight through his body. "My grandmother lived in Elk Springs. I used to come visit her, and it was an instant love affair between Montana and me. I moved to Elk Springs for a while four years ago, but

Whitehorn was a natural when Dakota Winston retired from the force. I love the size of the town, the location, the people, the mountain scenery surrounded by ranches... It's home for me now, the best I've ever known."

"No family here?"

Her low laugh filled the vehicle, an entrancing sound. David figured the lady might con a few criminals into surrendering just by seducing them with that laugh. "I have family everywhere," she confided. "Three brothers and four sisters. I don't remember a time in my life until now when I actually had a room to myself. Right now they're all scattered, but we keep in touch. We're as close as a phone or a modem or an airport can make us."

He eased back more fully into his seat, relaxing as he stretched his long legs out, pleased that she'd let down her barriers just for a moment.

"So now you know me," she said.

He had a feeling she'd just shown him the sheerest part of her surface, and that she didn't intend to show him much more. Gretchen Neal was cautious.

"And what about you?" she asked. "You're one of the Kincaids. Your family runs the Big Sky Bed & Breakfast. Your father is an architect. Your sister is a banker. One cousin runs a day care center. Your entire family is practically royalty in this town."

"We're just people, Gretchen."

The lady actually rolled her eyes. "You believe that, don't you?"

"It's true."

"David, after you left the station yesterday, every woman in the place was looking in the mirror, trying to see if she'd looked her best when you were there. This is not normal behavior around the station, in case you didn't know that. You're— Well, I'm sure you know what you look like and when you add that to the allure of being a Kincaid, that makes you a temptation to most of the women around here. Especially to those looking for husbands."

She sounded and looked somewhat flustered. David raised one brow. "Just most of the women? Gretchen, you wound me. Deeply."

Her chuckle tempted him to lean closer. "Sorry, I'm just…immune. Some of us are wedded and bedded to our jobs. Marriage isn't an option for me."

That got his attention. "So you're dead set against marriage. Interesting. Is it because of your job?"

She took one hand from the wheel and held it out, palm up. "Not really. And don't get me wrong. I like men just fine and I'm not anti-marriage. It's a perfect choice for some people, but it's not for me. I've already had my family, and while I adore every member of the Neal clan and I'd go out on the skinniest limb for any one of my brothers or sisters, I'm just not prepared to go that route again. I raised babies when I was still very young, I changed diapers, took temperatures, dried eyes and monitored curfew to help my mother out. Now I'm done with that. I like living alone and being free to make my own choices. And I intend to go on doing just that. I'm a lifer now, a loner. So don't get panicky, Hannon. The women in the station may bat their eyes at you and run to get you coffee if you purr at them, but you're safe from me."

He chuckled. "You may find this hard to believe, but in spite of being a Kincaid, I don't expect anyone, under any circumstances, to fetch coffee for me. And as for being safe from you, well…" He held out both hands. "Somehow I just wasn't all that worried that you were going to crawl across the gearshift and onto my lap."

David was surprised and entranced by the slight blush on her cheeks. She was tough, but not that tough. She didn't want to get married, and it sounded as if she had good reasons. He had some good reasons of his own, the chief one being that he'd been a loner way too much of his life to be real good at maintaining a relationship for very long, not to mention all the bad relationships he'd watched his friends get embroiled in. But marriage, a wife, kids, had a certain dreamlike fantasy appeal to him. He wished he had the ability to make a go of it. Unfortunately, he didn't. Besides, right now, there were more important things to consider.

"You think we've dropped enough barriers to enable you to trust me with a few of the details of the case now?" he asked.

Gretchen felt the low hum of David's voice go through her like a touch that could seduce every secret out of her. But of course, they were working together on this case. It was time to give her assistant some assistance.

"You know that a resort casino is in the plans, and that part of it is going to be built on Kincaid land?"

He nodded. "The land belongs to distant relatives. It's destined to be inherited by Gabriel Reilly Baxter, Garrett Kincaid's youngest grandson."

"Yes, the Kincaid portion, about fifteen acres, will house a hotel and spa, and the other half of the development being built on thirty acres of the Laughing Horse Reservation will consist of the casino as well as some honeymoon cottages up in the mountains. It's a joint venture, one that makes sense, I suppose. The Cheyenne provide land that can be used for a casino and the private investors chip in the funding. Lyle Brooks has rounded up some silent investors to finance the project, and Lyle's in charge of much of the operation. You're friends with him?"

David frowned. "Why do you say that?"

She shook her head, strands of her hair catching on her lips. She carelessly freed it and gave him a look. "Lyle's another distant relative, isn't he? Another Kincaid, a grandson of Garrett Kincaid's, and a member of the country club set I'm sure you belong to." She wanted to apologize for what had to sound like an accusation, but she had to place all her cards on the table.

"You could have mentioned those things to Rafe yesterday."

"Rafe knows what I know. It's obviously not a problem for him."

"And for you?"

She studied him, a small frown between her eyes. "It's just something that needed mentioning."

"No need to apologize," he said, even though she hadn't done that. "You're right. It needed mentioning. I suppose that's why Rafe put you in charge. You don't avoid the tough questions even though it would be easier to do so."

"No, I don't, but I do try to be fair." It was the best she could do. He needed to know that she would still be cautious, but that she would trust him as far as she could, given the circumstances.

"I'm beginning to see that, and I agree that you need to know more of my background. The fact is that Lyle and I don't share martinis at the country club. We come from two different sides of the family and until very recently, long after I moved away, Lyle's side lived completely in western Montana. I don't really know the man."

Gretchen gave him a nod. He supposed that meant that she trusted him a little bit anyway. Or maybe it merely meant that she didn't see any point in arguing about what she couldn't change.

He stared at her, trying to decipher that almost unreadable expression she worked so hard at maintaining.

"All right," he said. "So Lyle is heavily involved in the resort/casino deal and then a skeleton shows up when they begin to dig the hotel site. I've heard that much and also that there was a bullet lodged in the rib bone. The bones belong to Raven Hunter, a Native American who went missing from the reservation thirty years ago."

"A man who had made Jeremiah Kincaid angry by falling in love with Jeremiah's sister, Blanche," she added.

"You didn't add the obvious—that Blanche was my aunt and she died in childbirth. The baby she gave birth to is my cousin, Summer. It's an old story, one the Kincaids don't talk about too much. And now there's a body and an old murder to solve. Anything I should know that wasn't in the file?" David asked.

She shook her head. "We've already interviewed those people in the area who might have had a link to Raven in any way. Old friends, your mother, your aunt, people on the rez who came in contact with him. It's all there in black and white, what little there is. Right now the case is more or less on hold while we wait for

Jackson Hawk, the tribal attorney, to locate Storm Hunter, Raven's brother. We need to find out if Storm knows any more than we do about what happened all those years ago. But Storm's been gone from the area almost as long as Raven has."

David blew out a deep breath. "With the passage of time and the two principals both deceased, this case will be a challenge. And Peter Cook?"

"A construction worker," she explained. "It appears that he slipped and fell into the hole he'd dug. Until we know more, excavation has ceased completely."

"Any new leads coming in?"

She had to smile at that one. "Every day. Ghosts. Aliens. People who claim they were out walking their dog in the middle of nowhere and they heard a rustle in the bushes."

His smile indicated a knowledge of what she was talking about. He'd been doing this for a long time, too. "Any likely leads, I guess I should have said."

"Not yet."

But at that moment, the radio crackled and the dispatcher came on. An armed robbery in progress. Just outside of town on a road they'd passed minutes ago.

Gretchen spun the car around and headed for the scene.

A hundred yards from their destination, she slowed and David got out of the car. As she came around the side, he pinioned her with a look. "I'll go in through the back door," he said, his voice barely stirring the air. "Stay outside the front in case someone tries to make a run out that door." He moved silently back into the trees and toward the house.

Gretchen blinked. Obviously there was a problem

here with chain of command. But David was already moving and she would not risk his life by stopping to stamp her foot and assert her authority.

At least not this moment.

She pulled out her weapon and approached the house.

Two

It was broad daylight but the shades on the little cottage had been pulled, blocking out most of the sunshine. David slid up to the kitchen window and peered in, but the curtains covering the windows were too thick to see inside.

"Don't touch those. Go away from here. Leave me and my things alone," he heard an elderly woman plead.

The sound of shoes shuffling on a bare floor drifted out, followed by a loud cracking sound and a grunt.

The woman squealed and David shoved against the thin wood of the door, which fell open beneath his weight. His gun was drawn as he bulleted through the entrance. He hoped that Gretchen was armed and ready as he got his first glimpse of the big, beefy man whirling toward the front door where she would be waiting.

"Freeze. Police," David ordered.

The man spun around, hands high, his eyes rolling back in his head.

"Don't shoot," the man called as Gretchen came through the front door, holding him in the sights of her 9 mm.

"Thank goodness you're here," the elderly woman said. "I didn't know what to do when I heard someone in the house."

"Mr. Adkins?" Gretchen asked, slowly lowering her gun to her side.

The man hung his head. David looked at Gretchen. She motioned for him to put his gun away.

"He was stealing cookies I made for the church bake sale," the woman declared. "I had to slap his hands to make him drop them."

David looked down at the red prints on the man's wrists.

"I wasn't stealing anything," the old man said.

"You're in my house, aren't you?" the woman demanded. "And you're armed. You've got a big rock in your pocket. I saw you studying it like you were going to throw it at me."

Her words jarred something in David's memory. "Mr. Adkins? Earnest Adkins?"

When the man didn't answer, David looked to Gretchen, who nodded.

David let out a sigh. He gazed at the man he'd once known rather well. Time had made changes.

"That rock in your pocket," David said, moving in closer. "I don't suppose you had a particularly good reason for carrying it around, did you?"

The man looked up, his eyes not quite recovered from the fear of having two guns trained on him. He nodded slightly. "Of course I did. A man carries rocks for a reason. Good reason, too. Just look at this. Isn't it a beaut?" he asked, pulling the rock from his pocket.

David gazed down at what really was a fine specimen of milky dolomite. "Mr. Adkins used to teach science at the high school. He studies geology," David explained.

"He was still stealing my cookies," the lady mumbled.

"He came into your house?" Gretchen asked gently.

"Yes," both man and woman said at once.

"The door was open and a cat came in," Mr. Adkins said. "This lady had left the cookies on the ledge and that big cat was all set to help himself. I was simply moving them," he said indignantly.

"I don't see any cat," the woman whined. David didn't, either, but the slight itch behind his eyes told him that there was one nearby.

Gretchen must have sensed the cat's presence, too, because a small smile lifted her lips and she looked around as if she expected to find whatever she was searching for.

"Oscar," Gretchen suddenly called. A grumbly purr rolled out from behind the kitchen door. Gretchen pulled it back and the biggest, blackest cat David had ever seen strolled out, nose in the air.

"Your buddy?" David asked Gretchen, who was smiling at the cat.

"He gets around the neighborhood. Sometimes he gets into places he shouldn't be."

"The man still had a rock in his hand," the elderly woman stated.

"Always do," Earnest Adkins said. "Ask him," he said, motioning to David. "You're David Hannon, aren't you? I recognize you now that you've put the gun away."

"I was a member of the science club. I've still got a few rocks Mr. Adkins passed on to me when I was there. He's an expert in local rocks and minerals," David told the two ladies. "Not that it's any excuse for trespassing," he said firmly, frowning at Earnest. "Since you don't know Earnest, would it be safe to guess that you're new to the area?" he asked the woman.

The lady let out a sigh and nodded. "Just a couple of months. My husband died last year and I came here to start out fresh, to get away from the city. You—you were just saving my cookies from that cat?" she asked Mr. Adkins.

"Maybe I should have knocked first," he admitted, "but Oscar was moving pretty fast."

A slight blush rose on the woman's still-pretty face. "I suppose I should thank you, then," she said. "And apologize to the two of you," she told Gretchen and David. "I'm used to living in the city and that's made me too cautious, I guess."

David shook his head. "You were right to call when you felt threatened. It's always smart to be cautious, especially when there's an uninvited stranger in your house," he said, looking pointedly at Mr. Adkins, who mumbled another apology and gripped his rock more tightly.

"But this is embarrassing, now that I know the truth," the lady said. "What can I do to repay you two for taking the trouble to come over here?"

David knew the woman wouldn't be happy if he told her that he needed nothing, so he took the easy way out. "I'm sure I should just issue the standard 'No thanks necessary, ma'am,' but…what kind of cookies did you say those were?"

The ploy worked. The lady laughed. "Double chocolate chip, and yes, please have some. You, too," she said to Gretchen and Mr. Adkins. "It's the least I can do. It won't hurt me to bake another batch."

David hazarded a glance at Gretchen then. One brow was raised in a rather superior, knowing smile as if he'd just done something brilliant. And later, when they said their goodbyes and left the cottage headed for the car, she placed her hand on his arm.

"Thank you for being so gracious to her."

David pulled up short, staring down at the woman—the detective, he corrected himself—standing before him. He could feel the warmth of Gretchen's slender fingers through the layers of cotton shirt and sports jacket. It was a tantalizing feeling, knowing that only a few bits of cloth lay between his skin and hers. An inappropriate feeling, he reminded himself. They were partners. They needed to work together like a machine, not twine together like man and woman.

"She was uncomfortable. There was no need for that. If something real and dangerous should ever occur, I wouldn't want her to hesitate about calling the authorities," he said simply. "And let's face it, while I'm rather partial to Earnest, he can't be entering people's houses even to save their cookies from stray cats."

Gretchen nodded and they walked on, but once David had climbed back into the car, she didn't start the engine. Instead she turned to him.

"I appreciate the way you wrapped up this call," she said, "but I think we have a definite problem here, Hannon."

He turned and stared into a pair of stubborn green eyes. Her chin was up, her lovely lips were firm, her arms were crossed.

For five whole seconds they simply studied each other. Then he held up both hands. "You're upset that I invaded your territory. You want to lead."

"It's my job," she said simply. "I intend to do it and do it well."

He stared at her for a few seconds more.

"I'm sure you're used to calling your own shots," she said pointedly, "but—"

"I am," he agreed. "And I can't promise not to step on your toes from time to time, but I'll make an attempt not to overstep my boundaries too often. I'll do my best to try and curb my basic instincts from now on."

Gretchen took a long and audible breath, but she merely nodded.

"I'm sure we'll get the hang of this in time. It takes practice for partners to learn to work as one body."

He stared at her hard, the vision her words called forth lodging in his mind immediately. A woman, a man above her, thrusting into the softness of her body, making himself a part of her very being. The thought nearly made him groan, and he fought it. He labored to keep his breathing even as he watched the woman seated not two feet away from him.

As he studied her, her eyes suddenly widened slightly as if she'd read his thoughts. Her breathing picked up a tad, but she didn't drop her gaze from his. She sat as if frozen.

David struggled, pushing the temptation of the image of himself braced above Gretchen to the farthest corner of his mind. "I can't quite believe you said that," he finally managed to say, his voice quiet and reasonably controlled, an amused but still somewhat ragged smile on his lips.

"What?" The word was released on a breath. Gretchen sat up straighter, higher.

He smiled in earnest now. She knew darn well what he meant. "Gretchen, has it occurred to you that this is not going to be easy?"

She sighed slightly, rubbing at the frown that formed between her delicate brows. "I think that pretty much says it, yes," she agreed.

"Why do you think that is?"

"I suppose it's because I've been a rather reluctant participant in this partnership and also because you don't like taking orders from a woman."

He shook his head slowly. "I've worked with many women in many contexts. Taking my directives from a woman isn't a problem. Having a relationship with a woman isn't a problem. Generally speaking, I keep my private and public life separate."

"We're not going to have a relationship."

"Exactly."

She took a deep breath, waiting for him to finish.

"However," he continued carefully, "I think it's only fair to warn you that wrong and stupid and completely out of place as it may be, the fact that you are a fine detective hasn't quite made me forget that you're a desirable woman, as well."

She didn't move. She almost didn't appear to be breathing. But he saw her swallow, then blow out a long, slow puff of air.

"Why are you telling me this?" Her voice was low. Sexy. Suspicious.

He shook his head slowly. "I'm telling you because we *are* going to be working as partners. I'll trust you to protect my back. I want you to be secure in the knowledge that I intend to protect your life at all costs, but don't expect me not to react as a man to a woman if you're going to make provocative comments."

She stared at him for long seconds. Then she nodded slowly. "Fair enough. I'll try to think before I speak."

"And I'll try not to initiate any…unwarranted bodily contact."

"Yes," she said on a cracked whisper. "Touching wouldn't be smart. It would make working together very difficult. Impossible."

"I know that, and that's my point. Finding the thin line we need to walk in the middle of the road is going to be difficult, Gretchen. My fault. My apology."

"Maybe we shouldn't be working together at all."

"Maybe. Except this is your case, and I fully intend to be on it."

"Rafe might feel differently if he knew we were going to have problems."

"What are you going to tell him? That I'm having trouble keeping my lips away from those of his top detective?"

He wasn't even leaning close, but he could feel her presence as if she had wrapped herself around him. Her soap-clean scent enticed him. He forced himself to keep his hands at his sides.

"No. I wouldn't tell him that. What's between you and me is…between you and me, Hannon," she said, releasing another long breath. "We'll deal with it together. We'll work through it."

He raised his lips in the slightest of smiles. "I know women who would have been hyperventilating in a similar situation. You're an admirable lady, Gretchen."

"I'm a good detective, too, David."

"Never let anyone say any different. I liked the way you manhandled Earnest into repairing a few things around Mrs. Barton's house. A good solution for both of them."

She smiled. "You're not trying to flatter me, are you, David?"

He lifted one brow. "Detective Neal, you wound me. I was completely sincere."

"Thank you very much, then," she said, starting the car. "So, Agent Hannon, do you think it's possible that you're ready to take an order from me now that we've established a few truths between us?"

He held out his hands in defeat. She was being a good sport. He had laid his cards on the table in such a way that she might well have been flustered or angry. He had told her the truth, he'd gotten in her face and she was dealing with it, but she still hadn't given up one millimeter of her authority. He could see why Rafe had put her in charge.

"Just say the word, Gretchen."

"That's a lovely sound, David. Since you're being so cooperative, let's go get lunch at the Hip Hop Café. And no cookies for you, partner. You've had enough for one day."

David smiled at Gretchen's attempts to move the conversation onto a lighter plane.

"You're a hard woman, Gretchen Neal. A real tough lady."

"I am," she said more soberly. "And don't you forget it."

He wouldn't. For her sake and the sake of this case, he would do his best to forget that Gretchen was a woman and simply think of her as the partner who was going to help him crack the Raven Hunter case. He hoped something enlightening would happen very soon.

"Gretchen, are you sure the dress is going to fit by the time the wedding takes place? Maybe you should just come in for one more fitting just to be certain. The wedding's still a few weeks away."

Gretchen heard the rising panic in her friend Pamela's voice and did her best to try and put herself in her friend's shoes. No dice. Gretchen had been a bridesmaid more times than she had fingers and toes, but she never had been a bride and never would be, just as she'd told David yesterday. Still, she did want Pamela to be happy…

"Pam, I promise you this dress is absolutely going to fit. It fits right now and I'm the same size that I've been for the past ten years. Everything's going to be okay, hon. Really."

"Oh, Gretch, I'm sorry. It's just…I want everything to be so perfect. You know?"

"I know, Pam." And she did know that much. Enough of her friends and cousins and sisters had gotten married in the past few years for her to be very familiar with this need for the most beautiful, perfect day of all eternity. "And, Pamela?"

"Yes?"

"Everything is going to be just wonderful. You love Raymond, don't you?"

"Gretchen, you know he makes my sun rise every morning."

"And he loves you more than he loves anything else. More than baseball and basketball, which is saying quite a lot for a sports nut like Raymond."

Her friend giggled on the other end of the line. "All right, all that's true."

"Then what more can you ask for, Pamela? The day is going to be perfect even if it rains elephants from the sky. You're marrying the man of your dreams."

A long silence hung on the line. A nice silence.

"Pam?"

"You're right, Gretchen. It's going to be a wonderful day. Only one thing could make it more perfect."

Uh-oh. Gretchen had heard this line before. She knew just where her friend was headed.

"It's not going to happen, Pam. I've told all of you, I just don't want to get married."

"Not even if you met a special guy?"

"If I meet a special man, we'll date, we'll share our thoughts, we'll probably make love, but in time it's going to end. I'm just not cut out for husbands and babies. I like my job. I like my life. That's just not going to change. Nothing's going to change."

She was right about that. But it still meant that every time someone asked her to stand up in a wedding or to attend a wedding or even mentioned the words wedding or marriage or husband or children, all her friends and loved ones were going to wish she were different. They were going to try their best to get her to settle down and make them feel that at last she'd fit herself into the world the way they wanted her to fit.

But Pam wasn't talking. Perhaps she was getting the message. Finally.

"You're thirty-two, Gretchen. You want to be alone all your life?"

Gretchen couldn't help chuckling at that. "Pam, hon, I have seven brothers and sisters, more cousins than is probably legal, and friends all over the country. Almost all of them are generous and loving. Like you, Pamela.

They share their lives, their homes, and their children, and I absolutely love that. How could I be lonely? And why do I need to raise my own family when I can just share in everyone else's whenever I feel the need?"

"Gretchen—"

"Pam, stop. Right now. I'm so happy for you and Raymond. I'm glad you're getting married and living the life you want. Be happy for me, too. I have everything I could ever need or want."

More silence.

"Okay, Gretchen, I *am* happy for you. I'm truly happy if you really do have everything you want."

Gretchen felt herself relax a bit. She and her friend talked a few minutes longer, but when they finally hung up, a frown formed on Gretchen's face.

"I do have everything I want," she whispered. "But just once, just one time, I wish I could show up at a wedding with a man on my arm." She wouldn't, of course. Asking a man to travel any distance with her to a wedding implied a closeness that she just didn't want to encourage. She had enough trouble with men who thought dating a female detective meant a lot of things it would never mean. But wouldn't it be great to show up with a date? Maybe then all her friends and family would believe that she was truly happy living a life with no ties outside of work. All she needed was a little help from the right kind of man.

Unfortunately the right kind of man didn't exist in Whitehorn. The only way she was going to find a date for this wedding would be if one fell from the sky and disappeared just as quickly the day after the wedding.

Three

It was definitely good to be home, David thought, sitting on the long porch of the Big Sky Bed & Breakfast that night and gazing out at the tall pines that stretched away for miles. He, along with his mother and father had stopped by for an overdue reunion with the remaining members of the family, taking the short walk across the sloping lawns that separated their home from the Big Sky. Now evening had dipped the stars in silver and cast them out over the sky to shine down on the elegant old manor house where Celeste and Jasmine still lived and where so many guests had found peace and beauty.

"You missed this. At least a little, didn't you? Admit it, David," his sister Frannie said, leaning back in her husband Austin's arms and gesturing to the crowded porch where all the people he loved best were now gathered.

David drank in the scene and noted how relaxed his

sister seemed. At last. She clearly loved her husband. Marriage suited her. "I missed *you,* squirt," he told her. "Missed all the torment of having you chase after me."

"Humph," she said with a twinkle in her eye. "You and Cleo and Summer used to torment and tease Jasmine and me. Wasn't it true, Cleo?"

"Mmm, absolutely," her cousin said, linking her hand in her husband Ethan's as she nodded her agreement at Frannie. "And wasn't it tons of fun?"

Her chuckle floated out on the night and his cousin Jasmine joined in. "It *was* great fun."

"The best," Summer agreed. "Remember when David wrote a play for us and we insisted he play all the male parts?" she asked. She smiled up at her husband, Gavin. "David spent his life practically surrounded by women," she told him. "Must have been a bit harrowing at times."

"Or…maybe not," Gavin said, staring around at the quartet of beauties gracing the porch.

"It did have its moments," David admitted. "I got to meet any number of young ladies I might otherwise not have had access to. And you were all very understanding about being forced to share your space with a mere male."

"Was it a pain having to deal with all our feminine foibles?" Jasmine asked, prodding her cousin. "Be honest, David, now that we're all grown up."

He turned and smiled at her and marveled at what a lucky man he had been. "The truth, Jasmine? It was pretty great. We were all very close, and no, I didn't mind at all being the only guy other than Dad most of the time. You all spoiled me shamefully, you know."

"Like you didn't spoil us," Cleo drawled. "You did. You and Uncle Edward." She sat silent for a full five seconds. Then she raised her brows speculatively. "So which of our friends did you want to meet that you didn't tell us about?"

David ran one hand over his jaw, not bothering to hide his grin. "Well, let's see. I would have killed to have Edith Darrowby run her fingers through my hair when I was twelve."

Cleo crowed. "I seem to recall her doing that very thing on this front porch one summer when you were home on spring break."

David raised one brow and smiled. "My, what a good memory you have, Cleo, love."

"Yes," she said softly. "Considering how many women you've kissed, it's amazing I remember one specific lady. We've missed you, David. You kept us from getting too serious."

"And you were always ready to defend any of us even when we didn't deserve it," Frannie added. "We've all missed you, big brother. Don't stay away this long again," she said, rising to give David a hug.

He gently kissed her cheek, then took a quick step to open the door that his aunt was struggling through with cups and saucers. "Aunt Celeste, why didn't you tell me you were carrying that? I would have done it for you. Now come on, turn those things over to me."

Celeste gave him a long, patient look. "That's why I didn't tell you. I wanted you to have time to visit with the children. Besides, you know I'm as strong as they come, and your parents are helping me out in the kitchen. Edward is carting out the coffee and Yvette has the cookies. Now you just settle back this one night and let us all look at you and talk to you. Don't fuss over us, David," she said, gently slapping his hands away as she set down her burden.

"Yes, dear, don't fuss. Indulge tonight. You and Edward can go back to being the big, predatory protective males in the morning. You know we eat that stuff up," his mother said, offering her cheek for his kiss as she followed Celeste through the door.

"What's a guy to do?" David asked his father as Edward moved out into the night.

"Simple enough, son. Just enjoy being surrounded by the women who love him," Edward advised, setting down the urn he was carrying and wrapping his arms around his wife. "Just enjoy."

And he did, David thought later that night as he lay in bed. Now, as an adult, he could take pleasure in his family so much more than he'd been able to as a boy. Growing up, he'd been loved, he'd appreciated, but his illness had set him apart from the world in many ways. He'd wanted to be accepted the way other boys his age were, but he hadn't been able to do the things other boys had done. And so he'd retreated into solitude in public. He'd made himself a world within walls and only come out within the heart of his family. He'd even come to enjoy being a loner; he'd thrived on the solitude and the barriers he'd erected. But now?

"That's gone, that's done," he whispered. He didn't ever want to build those kinds of immovable walls again. He loved the world and being a part of it. He wanted all the joys of companionship and joining and belonging. Still, he knew there were flaws to parts of the plan. Years of holding himself aloof had taken their toll. He never dated a woman for long; he always had the urge to move on soon after the start of a relationship.

Secretly he might want to try for the kind of closeness and marriage his parents had, but he knew it was just the kid inside him still wanting something he couldn't have. The truth was that he would never allow himself to offer love or marriage to a woman. Not when he couldn't sustain the feelings a relationship needed to survive. Promising a woman his heart and then asking for it back just wouldn't be fair or right.

So, no, he didn't want to be a loner anymore, and yet in some ways he still was one and probably always would be. Maybe—just maybe—he and Gretchen Neal had something in common, after all.

"Whoa, hang on there. Gretchen, you're not going to tell me that this little scrap of fluff is actually *your* dog?" David asked the next day. He lifted his lips in a half smile as he followed Gretchen into the door of the small white cottage and was immediately assailed by a bit of white fur, big brown eyes and frantically wagging tail dancing around his feet. "I'm surprised. A tough lady like you. This little guy is not exactly standard-issue watchdog," he said, raising one brow.

Gretchen rolled her eyes. "I told you that you didn't have to come with me. I explained that I was perfectly capable of carrying in a bag of groceries on my own."

"In other words, uninvited guests have no right to insult your pet?" David asked with a grin, depositing the bag on the kitchen table and bending to scratch beneath the little dog's upturned chin.

"Exactly," Gretchen agreed, watching his easy way with her pet. "Goliath is a very intelligent creature. He knows when he's been insulted."

David looked down at the obviously eager wriggling of the pink-tongued little animal.

"Of course. I can see that. Looks really put out to me," he said with a wink at his new canine pal. David rose to his feet and looked at Gretchen, whose mouth was twitching in an obvious bid to hold back a smile.

"Well, he usually gets offended very easily," she insisted. "He doesn't ordinarily get this exuberant over some mere man walking through my door," she said, as if men were swinging through her door every darn hour of the day. The thought sent a small arrow of irritation spiraling through David. He thrust it aside. Gretchen was, after all, a splendidly lovely lady, and she was a woman working in a world filled with testosterone-laced males. It only stood to reason that she'd slayed her share of his own sex, and anyway, he had no business butting into that part of her life. He'd told her that he wouldn't.

"I'm sure you're right about your little friend here," David said with a nod. "I can see he's probably chewed up his share of male ankles. Probably only spared me because of the groceries I was carrying," he said. "But, Gretchen?"

"Hmm?"

"'Goliath'? You really call this little pretend puppy Goliath?" He looked pointedly downward and down farther still to the floor far below where the tiny white tail swished against his shoestrings.

She shrugged. "I thought he needed a little help. Everyone can't have the advantage of being tall and strong," she reasoned, looking pointedly at David.

"You thought he needed a little assist," he said, wondering if the lady knew just how much her words revealed about her. "Where'd you find him?"

Gretchen blew out a breath as she reached into the

first bag of groceries and pulled out a head of radicchio. "The humane society. I was looking for a Lab," she explained. "Or a Shepherd. Maybe a St. Bernard."

"Tough-guy dogs," he surmised.

"Well, yes. Why not?"

"Absolutely. Smart dogs to keep around."

"I know, but then—"

"Goliath looked at you with those big caramel-brown puppy-dog eyes that said 'I need help.'"

Gretchen glanced back over her shoulder and leveled a long cool green-eyed stare at him. "Believe me, I'm not such a pushover as that, Hannon. You don't work the streets of Miami and survive if you fall for every pair of big beautiful eyes that look at you beseechingly."

"I'm sure you don't," he said, moving up behind her. He wondered just what all she'd seen in those years in the city. He was pretty sure much of it had been ugly. There was a telling tiny scar on her wrist and one just beneath that firm little chin of hers. Maybe from falling off a bike as a kid—or maybe from having a knife held a bit too close for comfort. Any way he looked at it, he was positive that she'd learned the survival skills every cop in that sort of situation had to learn. Emotional retreat. Develop a tough patina. Never get too involved. She had those eyes that looked right through a man to read secrets he didn't want read. She had that closed-off look she could turn on whenever she needed to. And yet... He looked back down to the tiny dog worrying a rubber bone as if the chew toy were a criminal Goliath was trying to cuff.

"They were going to put him down. He was too frantic, too untrainable for most people," she explained apologetically. "It was probably foolish for me to take him, but—" She lifted a shoulder in a helpless gesture.

"You did what you felt you had to do," David said, holding out a box of rice to Gretchen, trying to ease her out of her discomfort by returning to the mundane task at hand. She took the box from him, her fingers brushing against his. Cool satin licking against his skin. At the stroke of her bare flesh against his, he felt a slight tremble go through her—and felt his own answering tremors deep inside. Unusual for him, he thought for about the fiftieth time since he'd met the woman. He always kept things light, easy. It was the way he liked things, the way things suited him, but he was relatively sure that nothing was going to be easy with Gretchen—on any level. She had too much to prove where he was concerned, too many barriers. One of those sprang up now. He knew when she made the effort to control that trembling his unexpected touch had brought on. She was right. It wouldn't do for the two of them to mix up the personal and the professional. They'd already discussed that issue.

And so he withdrew his hand, ended the contact that sent sensation in a warm arc through his body. He resisted the impulse to move closer, to step right into her space and drag her body up against his in a long, slow slide. He turned away and helped her finish shelving the groceries.

For long, languid seconds there was only the sound of cans clicking against cans, the whoosh of boxes being slid into place on the wooden shelves.

"David?" she finally asked.

He looked up and met the question in her eyes.

"Do you really think you can remain objective when this case is so tied into your own family?"

His brows drew together. He knew she had the right to ask although she'd already asked the question once before. It was a question that bore repeating given the gravity and the sensitive nature of the situation. Indeed, she had the obligation to demand the truth from him considering her responsibilities. But he knew her question was intended to raise a personal barrier as well as a professional one. She was letting him know that while he affected her breathing, she wasn't going to let it matter.

"I'm a firm believer that the truth frees people," he said. "I may not like the answers we discover, but I'll do my best to make sure that we do, indeed, discover the whole truth. You'll have my full cooperation no matter what. You can trust me, Gretchen."

But he could see that there was still uncertainty in her eyes. There would probably always be uncertainty there until he could prove—if he could—that he meant what he said. She was wishing she had been sent any other man than him. Still, she took a deep breath and looked away.

"Down, Goliath. Sit," she said softly but firmly when the little dog hopped around David, hoping for another chin scratching.

The dog immediately whimpered, but he did as he was told.

"I thought you said he was untrainable," David said.

She shook her head. "I said that he was considered untrainable. I happen to believe that anything is possible if a person is determined enough."

He smiled. "And yet you're working with me when that really wasn't what you wanted. You think you're going to be rid of me?"

She smiled sweetly. "You don't live in Whitehorn anymore, David, do you? Don't you think that if I really want to be rid of you, all I have to do is wait?"

David felt the impact of her smile—of her words—like a ball peen hammer to the chest. He forced a mock-sweet smile to his lips. "Ah, Gretchen, my dearest detective, what a wonderful, ripping way you have with words. Tears at a man's heart just to hear you speak."

She smiled back ever so innocently. "Oh, partner, I'm so glad we understand each other so well. Your candor is refreshing. Still, it's late and we have lots of miles to cover in the morning, so go home now. I wouldn't want to have to sic my attack dog on you."

David looked down at Goliath, who was still obediently sitting.

"She's pretty bossy, isn't she, buddy? Guess I'd better get out of here before she starts ordering me to sit, too." The little dog whimpered and wiggled slightly, obviously wanting a goodbye pat but not willing to leave his post.

Gretchen looked at the two doleful males in front of her and let out the grin she'd been holding back.

"All right, Goliath. Go ahead," she said with a small shake of her head.

The little dog bounded over for a touch from David and received what he was looking for.

"You need some male companionship, buddy, you let me know," David said. "Or maybe some tips on how to worm your way past some bigger dog into a lady's heart."

"David," Gretchen drawled as the maddening man raised his brows and gave her that warm seductive smile she was beginning to know too well. Really, this man was just way too smooth for her to ever feel restful in his presence. He'd obviously been born to reel women in with just a look.

"Gretchen," he drawled, imitating her tone. "Tomorrow I want to see the construction sites where the bodies were found. We'll go right after morning coffee at the Hip Hop Café."

She nodded before she realized he was calling the shots again. Automatically she opened her mouth to protest.

He tilted his head slightly and gave her a serious, questioning look with those deep emerald eyes of his that sent a spark zipping through her entire body.

"Yes?" he asked, his voice low and sexy.

He was playing a game with her. She knew that. She could either fall into the trap by arguing with him or she could refuse to play. Gretchen was absolutely positive that David was a master at the game of winning a woman's attention. She was good at what she did, but so was he. And she was in way over her head right now in this cozy space with David Hannon's broad shoulders filling up her kitchen and her vision.

Shaking her head, she dismissed the subject. "Thank you," she said instead. "For carrying in my groceries."

"Thank *you*," he whispered back.

Confusion had her opening her eyes wider.

"For taking in a sickly little runt even though I know darn well he wasn't what you really wanted. Even though you were probably kicking yourself all the way home, and he's probably caused and will continue to cause you no end of trouble."

Gretchen was pretty sure they weren't really talking about Goliath anymore.

"I can handle trouble, David. I welcome trouble."

He grinned again, then moved out the door and pulled it almost shut behind him. "That's good, Gretchen," she could swear she heard him say just before the door clicked shut.

She couldn't help smiling. She couldn't help wondering why her skin felt alive and tingling even though the only touch she and David had shared had been slight and over too quickly. But there was something about the lazy way the man looked at her, that made her feel that he had touched her time and time again. There was something about the quiet, deep tone in his voice when he said her name, that made her feel he'd been thinking about what it would be like to slide his naked skin over hers.

"The man is definitely right," she whispered to no one in particular. "It's a good thing you know how to handle trouble, because top-notch agent though he may be, David Hannon is going to be a major source of very deep trouble."

And as she climbed into bed that night, another thought traipsed through her consciousness. It was a good thing she'd never taken a man like David to one of her friend's or relative's weddings. He was just the kind of man that would make people start urging her to think seriously about getting married lest she fall prey to some dangerous man with hot eyes and hot lips and deliciously seeking hands.

Maybe someday, she thought, she'd find the right man to haul off to one of those weddings. For now, though, she had to think about taking David off to examine those construction sites.

They had two bodies on their hands—and no answers to their questions.

* * *

They had barely gotten their coffee at the Hip Hop the next morning when Lily Mae Wheeler called across to their table.

"David, how are your parents? And your aunt? Your sister and your cousins? And those nice young men Cleo and Frannie married? I haven't been out to the Big Sky in a billion years."

David did his best not to laugh as the elderly lady leaned forward more and more with each question. The long bright dangling beads that dripped from her ears shook with each movement, but even more amusing was the fact that his mother had just been complaining that Lily Mae had been out to the Big Sky way too much lately. Her excuse was that she was checking up on the family and the newlyweds, but Yvette was sure that Lily Mae just wanted the latest dirt on what had happened between Jeremiah Kincaid and Raven Hunter thirty years ago.

"Everyone is doing great, Lily Mae," he said gently, all too aware that half of the lady's nosiness stemmed from the fact that she was alone after being widowed and then divorced twice after that. She could be a wicked gossip and cruel, but at the heart of all of that was a kind of pathetic need to be the center of attention. He knew that, but it didn't mean he was sharing any information the lady didn't need to know. Such as the fact that his aunt was so worried about this case that lately she could be heard quietly pacing the floor on certain dark and lonely nights. "The Big Sky has its usual complement of summer customers out to view the beautiful Montana scenery."

"You obviously love the view, too," Lily Mae said,

shaking her head. Her glow-in-the-dark temporarily red hair, unlike her earrings, was wrapped around her head and therefore immobile. "How can you stand to live in the city after growing up out here?"

"I miss it every single day, Lily Mae," David said quietly, and he was surprised to realize how much he meant that. Not that it mattered. His work was important to him, and his work was elsewhere, but there was something about home…

"The city's not so bad, Lily Mae." Gretchen's soft voice brought him out of his reverie. He turned to look into her determined green eyes over her coffee cup. He wondered if she meant what she said, or if she was trying to defend him from Lily Mae. A touching thought. Probably not true, however. More likely Gretchen Neal was simply trying to convince him that he'd be better off scurrying back to Atlanta as soon as possible.

"Well, you grew up in the city and yet here you are," Lily Mae argued. "Although I hear you're taking a trip to Helena soon."

Gretchen froze. A small, almost imperceptible groan slipped through her lips, and she had an undeniable urge to reach across to Lily Mae's table and shove the words back into her mouth. How had the woman found out? And why did she care that Lily Mae knew?

"A bridesmaid again?" the woman was saying, shaking her head sadly. "How many times does that make now?"

Gretchen looked into the eyes of her friend Emma who was waiting on the next table. "I'm sorry," Emma mouthed, and was instantly forgiven. Gretchen knew all too well how good Lily Mae was at worming secrets out of people.

She somehow managed to smile at Emma and shrug her shoulders. But it was difficult. She knew Lily Mae's condescending tone too well. She'd heard it from any number of people lately. As if everyone thought she couldn't get a man of her own. As if they didn't understand that she just didn't want to get married. Ever.

"I've rather lost count of how many weddings I've stood up at, Lily Mae," she said, telling the truth. "I guess I'm just lucky, though, to have so many friends who love me enough to want me to be a part of their weddings."

She managed to keep the defiance out of her voice. She managed to keep from even looking toward David. It didn't matter that it was her own choice not to wed. People looked at the fact that she had stood up at so many weddings as somehow humiliating. *She* didn't feel that way. She loved celebrating with her friends and family, but she hated that pitying tone people like Lily Mae sent her way. She hated knowing that even those closest to her worried about the fact that she was a perpetual bridesmaid well on her way to living her life alone forever.

"I'm sure you're right, dear," Lily Mae said, patting Gretchen's hand. "But it's a shame you haven't gotten married yourself, Gretchen."

"Lily Mae," David drawled. "Bite your tongue, sweetheart." David's voice was low and sexy as he leaned forward, close enough so that Gretchen could feel the warmth of his skin next to hers. "If Gretchen had gotten married, she would have ruined the nighttime dreams of half the men in this town."

Gretchen sucked in a deep breath of air. She saw Lily Mae's eyes go wide. The woman leaned closer. "What do you mean, David Hannon?"

He gave the lady a slow, sexy smile. "I mean, Lily Mae, that there are a substantial number of male animals in this town who moan in their sleep over restless dreams of Gretchen Neal. There's just something about a woman who's good at her job, who knows what she wants and doesn't want, and who happens to be beautiful, as well, that makes a man feel kind of crazy on a dark and lonely night. Something irresistible. It gives a man a goal, something to warm himself with in the winter and hold close to him in the summer. The way I look at it, Gretchen is performing an important civic duty by keeping the hopes and dreams of all of us single males alive. It makes a man sit up a little straighter and behave a bit better if he knows that a woman like Gretchen may pass by at any moment. If she were already married, well, she'd be some other man's woman and we wouldn't care so much. I'm sure the crime rate in town might take a small leap or two."

Gretchen realized that the whole café had gone quiet and that Lily Mae still hadn't answered. It was the first time in a long time that anyone had stunned the woman into silence.

"Now if you'll excuse us, Lily Mae, Gretchen and I have some important business to attend to. The woman is leading a criminal investigation, you know. She doesn't have time today to think about getting married."

"No, of course not," Lily Mae finally said, placing her long, ring-covered fingers against her chest. "Gretchen's going to find the murderer who still might be on the loose. I only mentioned marriage because I thought Gretchen would make some man very happy."

"Thank you, Lily Mae," Gretchen said, going along because she knew deep in her heart that the woman didn't really mean to be cruel. "I'm sure you'll make some man happy again, too, someday. You're a much better cook than I am. That's for sure."

The woman beamed. She didn't even seem to notice that David and Gretchen, her audience, had gotten up and were walking toward the door.

Gretchen was all the way back to the car and seated before she turned to David. "Thank you for saying all that, even if it was a little embarrassing and absolutely untrue."

He turned to her and smiled that melting smile. She was almost getting used to the way her breath came too hard and fast by now.

"It was the least I could do for my partner," he said quietly, brushing aside her gratitude.

"I did feel like I had a partner back there," she admitted.

"You do."

"Yes, I guess I do," she said, starting the car and pulling out into traffic.

"And, Gretchen?"

"Yes, David?" She kept her eyes on the road and the contented smile on her lips.

"For the record, I meant what I said back there about you not letting other people influence what you do. You're a strong, independent woman and you know your own mind and what you feel is best for you."

"Thank you, David. I'd say you're rather strong and independent, too."

She could almost feel his grin. "That's been said about me. Yes, it has," he agreed. "And Gretchen?"

She took her eyes off the road and turned to him just for a second. His eyes were narrowed, intent on her own eyes…and lips. Especially on her lips. She took a deep breath and grasped the wheel harder as she looked away.

"I meant every other word I said, too," he repeated. "Any man who spends any time with you and doesn't imagine you naked in his arms at night is lying."

His words made her voice freeze in her throat. She should remind him that they were working together on a case, that he was assisting her. She should tell him that what he was saying was inappropriate for the situation.

"And any woman who looks into those bedroom eyes of yours and doesn't see a bed at her back would be less than truthful, too," she heard herself saying instead. But when she turned and saw the lazy intent in those very same eyes, she shook her head. "But now that we've both admitted that we're attracted, David, I think we'd better also both agree that it would be all wrong for us to act on our desires. We do have to work together, after all, and I'm sure you've got plenty of women waiting for you back in Atlanta. You want to get this case solved, after all, don't you?"

His smile was slow when it came, laced with sex appeal and the danger that was an inherent part of his life. "You're a very wise and perceptive lady, Gretchen Neal. I do want to solve this case."

"Then let's do it," she agreed, wishing her words hadn't been so shaky. Because for all that she knew she was right and staying away from David Hannon's body was the only way they could operate together, there was a part of her that had been unleashed today. She wondered how long it would take her to banish the vision that had formed in her mind, of David braced above her as he lowered himself and joined his body to hers.

* * *

"This is where Raven Hunter's remains were found," Gretchen said, carefully skirting the yellow police tape that protected the area from further contamination. "They had spent two weeks clearing the land when his bones were discovered. Until then no one had known exactly what had happened to him. Even now, with a bullet in his ribs, we can't be sure whether he was killed on this site or whether his body was brought here after his death. With Storm away, we don't know much about what happened in the last few hours he was alive."

"But we do know that he and Jeremiah had not been on good terms. Jeremiah had tried to pay him to leave town and desert my aunt Blanche. Everyone had assumed that he'd left town right after that."

"That part of the story is pretty well documented, yes."

"And no other evidence was found other than the bullet wedged into the rib. No weapon. No other clues that we could use."

"There were rocks found over the skeleton. More than there were on the rest of the site. Possibly intentionally placed there. But then, you know that already. You've read the file. The area's been thoroughly searched."

"I know. I'm just wondering what might have been damaged or missed in those first few days when the digging was going on, if there were any clues that might have been lost that could still be recovered."

She shrugged her agreement. "We'll keep trying. In the meantime, all we can do is wait for Storm to show up so we can interview him."

"How about the other site? What do you know about the Peter Cook case?"

"At this point we don't suspect foul play. The evidence indicates that the man died in a fall at a site where he had every reason to be. And there were no witnesses that we've been able to locate."

She stopped, but apparently she hadn't stopped soon enough. David's brows rose.

"You don't suspect foul play, but you're not completely sure this is a case you can close without nosing around a bit?"

She shook her head as David waited for her answer. "It's nothing, really. Absolutely nothing that would ever matter in a legal sense. Just a strange feeling. Peter Cook was an experienced outdoorsman."

Nodding, David acknowledged her doubts. "Not the kind to slip under normal circumstances?"

She shrugged. "Everyone has accidents now and then. Still, I do have a disturbing feeling about all of this."

"Who wouldn't? There *have* been a number of strange events taking place in Whitehorn in the past few years," David conceded. "Murders. Kidnappings. Far too many for a town this size. I thought all that was done, that all the pieces had been tied up tight, but now here we have it. A thirty-year-old murder and another death, both on Kincaid land. More trouble on the home front."

"I'm sorry your family has gone through so much," Gretchen said gently, and David was sure she meant what she said.

He shook his head. "Don't feel sorry for us, Gretchen. We're a happy bunch, for the most part. But this has got to affect Summer to some extent. She lost her mother a few weeks after she was born and thought that her father deserted her. Now there are questions about Raven to be answered and all the upheaval of reliving the antagonism between her father and her uncle, but Summer's very happy now that she's married Gavin. He'll help her deal with this. It's Aunt Celeste I'm worried about. She's just not well. This is taking too much of a toll on her."

"We'll solve it, David. Together. How can we miss? The FBI's finest and Whitehorn's first lady of crime fighting?"

He looked up at her from where he was down on one knee, studying the dirt that had beheld so many secrets over the years. Behind her, the beautiful snow-covered peaks of the Crazy Mountains rose up. The picture was breathtaking. A beautiful, intelligent, determined woman standing against a backdrop that radiated strength and vitality and endurance.

"How can we lose, partner?" he agreed. "A team like us is bound to get at the truth in time."

He rose to his feet and stood beside her. She held out her keys. "You drive today," she said. "I'm tired."

He looked down into eyes that were alive and alert.

"What you are, lady, is a liar. A lovely, generous liar. And fair. Very fair."

"Remember that when I get bossy next time."

He chuckled as he turned the key in the ignition and roared off down the road, headed toward town.

In the trees not far away from where Gretchen and David had been standing only moments ago, a thin man with dark hair and dark eyes watched them drive away. The cut of his suit was expensive, his tie was neatly knotted, and the look in his eyes was deadly, like a diamondback rattler's on the verge of striking.

"You two think you make such a perfect pair," he said, "but you don't know a thing. Not a thing. Only I know what really happened on this site. Only I know about the sapphires and Peter's disappearance, and only I will ever have the right to know. And the right to claim."

Oh, yes, he had been the forgotten one. His grandfather had turned all that good land over to all those illegitimate grandkids his uncle had begotten. Garrett Kincaid had all but forgotten Lyle Brooks was his grandson, giving him only one puny piece of land that skirted the reservation—and only after he and his mother raised a ruckus. But this piece, little Gabriel's piece, held such secrets. Rich secrets. Sapphire blue secrets. And he, Lyle Brooks, was going to own them, lock, stock, and barrel. He was, and no frigid ice queen of a lady detective was going to stop him. He would do what he had to do to maintain his secrets. After all, after a man had committed murder, he had nothing left to lose and everything to gain. And Lyle Brooks most certainly intended to gain whatever he could in any way he could.

Four

"So you were out walking your dog at six in the morning and you saw something suspicious, Mrs. Adams? How exactly would you describe what you saw?" David watched Gretchen as she stood the next day, her notepad in hand, her sunglasses pushed back on her blond hair, waiting patiently for the agitated woman to answer.

"Well, of course, I know how to describe it, Gretchen. It was that Mr. Babbins down the road. He was picking up his newspaper and he was looking at me real creepy."

"Did he say anything to you? Do anything?" Gretchen's green eyes told nothing of her thoughts. She simply continued to wait for the woman's response.

"No, he just…looked. But he's pretty old, Gretchen, old enough to have been around here thirty years ago. A person worries when bodies start turning up, you know."

"I know, Enid, but you don't have to worry. We're on the job policing the town. We're looking out for your safety. As for Mr. Babbins, I can't arrest him for a look. You know that. I believe he filed a complaint about your dog trampling his lawn a couple of weeks ago. Have you spoken with him about that?"

"Of course I have. I told him that my Buster has no interest whatsoever in his lawn. That man needs a life. He moans over that little bit of grass as if it were a child."

"Maybe it is like a child to him, Enid. His family's all grown up and moved away. His wife passed away years ago."

"I know. I know. But he *was* looking at me funny. If Jeremiah doesn't turn out to be the killer, no offense to you, Mr. Hannon, I'd start looking there at Mr. Babbins. Right down the block from my house. He might have other bodies under that lawn of his. Maybe that's why the grass is so green."

"I'll keep a record of your report, Enid," Gretchen promised as she and David bid the lady goodbye and went on their way.

"That's the fourth false lead we've had this week," David said, shoving his hand back through the heavy dark satin of his hair.

"Poor baby," she said, scribbling on her clipboard. "You must be missing the danger and excitement of the Bureau. Terribly."

He chuckled. "Still trying to get rid of me, Gretch?"

She shook her head. "No, actually, I really was feeling sorry for you. This must be a bit boring compared to your usual lifestyle."

"You think watching you twist the citizens of White-horn around your finger could ever be boring? You impress me, lady. Lots of people wouldn't have been nearly as patient with someone who just wants to complain about a troublesome neighbor."

"No, it's more than that. Everyone's worried since all these strange things have been happening. There's an edginess to the town. Enid was just nervous, and now that she feels she's done something positive, now that someone from the department has come out, listened to her and offered her some assurance, she'll feel a little bit better. It's part of the job, letting people know that you're out there trying to keep the lid on. Doesn't matter whether it's Miami or Montana. That's what people really want to know, that the people in charge of their safety are aware of their existence."

David watched her as she spoke. Her face was aglow with true satisfaction. She clearly loved her work. He wondered how she'd look if she felt that same kind of enthusiasm for a man, then shook his head at his own nonsense. He'd promised himself he wouldn't go down that road. But he was just about to ask her about her work in Miami when the radio came to life.

"Fifty-two. Domestic in progress at the Sadine place. Neighbors report suspect was yelling and shooting his gun into the trees. When the ammo gave out, he dropped it. No other known weapons. Both parties are in the living room. Entry should be no problem."

"Copy that. Fifty-two en route," Gretchen said, spinning out onto the road. Her voice was tight and hard and she spared David a glance after she'd asked the dispatcher for details. "You ever get involved in a domestic?"

"Not in my line."

"Ugly stuff," she said. "I did a lot of that in Miami. Not much around here, but it happens. Wayne Sadine doesn't get drunk often, but when he does, he likes to hit. He doesn't care who, but if his wife doesn't get out of his way, sometimes she's the one his fists make contact with."

The words came out sharp and clipped. David felt the muscles tighten in his jaw. He remembered Wayne and he also remembered the tiny woman he'd married.

But when they reached the small, crooked house, Gretchen exited the car like an Amazon intent on eating Wayne Sadine's liver for lunch.

The house was silent. She knocked, then turned the knob as a yell and a slap sounded inside.

Wayne turned and roared as David pushed in front of Gretchen, ready to take the brunt of any blows, but Gretchen was having none of his interference.

"Wayne, you're drunk," she said.

"It's my own house."

"Peggy's house, too. What happened, Peg?"

It was obvious he had hit her, but the woman stood silent.

"Peggy?" Gretchen said gently.

"You know what will happen if you take him in."

"I know we can keep him until morning. He's drunk, he's disorderly, and not only did he hit you, but he was out in the road earlier firing a weapon. The neighbors called in the complaint and they're not going to back down. At least he'll be sober by morning. At least he'll know he can't just keep doing this and getting away with it."

But of course, David knew, the man could get away with it if Peggy didn't walk away from him, and it was just as clear looking at her that she was much too scared to do that.

"Come on, Peg," he said gently. "Let me take you over to the Big Sky for the night. You remember my mother—don't you?—when your mother used to work there. She always liked you. Said you had pretty strawberry hair."

"Don't touch my wife," Wayne roared, and David felt a prickle at the back of his neck. He whirled just in time to see Wayne hurtling his way and Gretchen crouching and kicking her leg up right into Wayne's path. The man fell like a tree that had been neatly sawed in two.

David stared down at the slender woman who had saved his back. He automatically reached to scoop her up, then changed course and gave her his hand for an assist when he realized what he was doing. No way would Gretchen appreciate being treated as if she were a delicate flower, nor should she be treated that way. The woman had just acted with a speed, an agility and a courage and decisiveness that many big brawny men could never have matched.

Grasping her narrow hand, David gave a tug, bringing her back to her feet. He managed to stop himself from pulling her to him, but he knew that the look he gave her was fierce and tight and appreciative.

She stared at him, sucked in a long deep breath, then turned her attention to Peggy.

"I'll read Wayne his rights and give him a bed for the night when he wakes up," she promised the woman, brushing her disheveled hair back from her brow. "Could I talk you into pressing charges?"

Peggy shook her head. "I know it's cowardly, but I—I just don't think I can do that."

Gretchen opened her mouth, then shut it again. Clearly she and Peggy had walked this path before.

"About the Big Sky," David began, holding out his hand to Peggy.

"No, I couldn't. Your mother wouldn't even know I was coming."

He tilted his lips up slightly. "We'll call her," he whispered conspiratorially. "She'll rush around getting ready for you and be pleased as can be that she's going to get a chance to visit with you. Since your mother passed away, she hasn't had a chance to talk to you."

"Oh, I don't think—"

But some of the hesitation had drained away from her eyes.

"Don't think. Let me call."

And so they stayed. David heated water and Gretchen made tea while they brought Wayne around, then read him his rights.

Edward and Yvette drove up just at that moment.

"David, love," Yvette said. "I'm glad you called. And, Gretchen, I hear you decked him. Good for you. I hope he has a knot on his head to match the ones he must have been born with. Imagine beating on my poor little Peggy. Come here, sweetheart. We're getting you back to the Big Sky and into a nice crisp nightgown and a big feather bed."

David's mother bustled around like a mother hen. David gave Gretchen a knowing look and took charge of Wayne.

"Hit him again, dear, if you need to. I don't want him getting anywhere near Gretchen with those fists" were his mother's last words as she and her husband pulled away with Peggy in tow.

He and Gretchen watched them drive away, then led

a limping Wayne to their own car. David turned to Gretchen as they clicked the door shut behind the man.

"That was an impressive kick back there, lady. You get to put those moves to use a lot back in Miami?"

He could see by the flash in Gretchen's eyes and the sag in her shoulders that the overly long day was taking its toll on her. She was both charged up and tremendously tired.

"He was going for your back, Hannon. He had a bottle poised over your head," she said with a sigh. "I didn't have time to think."

"I know," he said quietly. "I could have twisted away, but not with Peggy standing right behind me. Thank goodness for those long, delicious, and very talented legs of yours, Officer Neal. Now, should we get this mess in the back seat into town and a jail cell?"

"Good idea," she agreed. "Almost as good as handing Peggy into your mother's care. That was generous and sweet of both of you."

"My mother is a very generous woman, Gretchen, and with her children grown, she misses taking care of people—except for my father, of course. The B and B helps, but most of her visitors are just passing through. She hasn't gotten to put those deep-seated nurturing skills to use nearly enough to suit herself lately. I'm hoping it will be good for both her and Peggy."

And with that, he gently disentangled the keys from Gretchen's fingers. "You watch Wayne," he said, not wanting her to know that he needed to coddle her a little now that the adrenaline was draining out of her.

She chuckled. "Very smooth, David. I can see that you're used to taking care of the women in your life, but I'm an officer. I can handle stress and fatigue."

"Mmm, I know that. But why should you have to now that you have a partner to share that stress and fatigue with you? Go on, now. I'll let you be the strong one again tomorrow. For now, just watch Wayne."

Hours later when all the paperwork had been done and Gretchen had gone home, David kicked his feet up on the desk and leaned back in his chair. He was glad his mother had come for Peggy. She'd done so much worrying about his aunt Celeste lately that having Peggy around would be a comfort and a distraction for her and hopefully would be a brief respite for Peggy, as well.

He'd wished to relieve some of the stress and tension his family was going through by helping to bring a hasty end to this case, but it was clear nothing hasty was going to happen here. Raven and Jeremiah were both dead and Storm seemed to have vanished into the past, as well. The mystery was still a mystery and David chafed at his inability to break through the mist that surrounded it. As for this current situation with Peggy, well, it was a help of sorts. His mother was quite simply never happier than when she could bustle around helping a young person find a way in the world. It would be a distraction for her.

But what about him?

David groaned and ran his hands over his eyes, trying to dislodge the picture of Gretchen throwing herself in front of Wayne today, that long elegant leg shooting up to catch him just beneath the chin.

How could a man resist that?

"Resist," he ordered himself. The lady has her life set just the way she likes it and so do you. All those hot thoughts coursing through you are nothing more than that. Ticklish desires. Fantasies. Just like the ones he'd had as a kid. Of playing football back in the days when his body wouldn't allow him to do much of anything he'd wanted it to do. He'd learned early on that he was a kid who wasn't going to be able to run with the pack. He was going to have to go his own route, forge his own trails. And it didn't matter that things had changed once he'd grown healthier and he'd become much taller and stronger than anyone would ever have believed. Some things just shouldn't be approached. Things that added complications to an already complicated situation. Such as touching Gretchen.

The ringing of the phone sent his fretful thoughts flying. "Hannon," he said as he snagged the receiver and brought it to his ear.

"David, how's it going?"

"Sascha? What are you up to, buddy?"

"A guy can't check up on his best friend? His friend who hasn't even called to say hello?"

David smiled to himself.

"Depends on the reason why he's checking up. The last time I saw you, you told me you were living in Bridget Nelson's bed. I thought I might be interrupting something important if I called."

"Good point," his friend said with a deep chuckle. "But right now the lady's asleep and I've been hearing rumors about what's going on in Whitehorn."

"Rumors?"

"Hey, news travels fast. If you can't find info in the Bureau, where can you find it? I hear you've paired up with a career detective. A lady. A very by-the-book lady."

"Gretchen's very talented," David said with a lazy smile. "Anything more you want to know about her?"

"She succumb to your charms yet like almost all the other women I've met?"

"Sasch?"

"Uh-oh. I hear 'back off' in your voice."

"Very good. I knew we were friends for a reason. You know when to butt out."

"You never used to get so upset when I asked about your current lady."

Sascha was right and David was pretty sure he knew the reason. The reason was that Gretchen was not his current lady and wasn't going to be his lady at all.

"She that special, David? You know what I've told you about getting in too deep. Take it from a man who knows way too much about what can go wrong when that happens. And you should know. You were the one who kept me alive when I was going through my divorce."

David felt a frown forming between his eyes. He *did* remember just how broken his friend had been. He and Sascha Fitzgibbons were a lot alike. Men with warm families, but essentially men who trod their own road. Alone. It was the truth. It was why he'd never even told Sascha that sometimes late at night when he was tired, he wished he were different, wished he had the ability to try for a lasting and permanent connection. He didn't. Women were his for the taking much of the time, but once taken, he seemed to tire quickly. Knowing that about himself, he tried not to get too close to any one woman. Not close enough to burn her, anyway.

"David, you're not falling for this Gretchen, are you? You've only known her a week."

A long, tired sigh slipped through David's lips.

"It's not like that, Sasch. Gretchen is simply a very good detective and a very nice lady."

Silence, then a low whistle.

"And there's nothing more to say than that, Sasch. You got that? I don't want any rumors flying around the office about Gretchen, okay? She doesn't deserve that kind of treatment."

"I hear anything, David, the guy who says it will be eating the carpeting on the floor."

David laughed. Sascha was the biggest pussycat he knew. A giant of a man and as gentle as they came. He hated hurting people. That didn't mean that he couldn't fight with the best of them, but he very rarely needed to.

"Thanks, Sascha, and thank you for worrying about me, but I'm all right. I'm technically on leave, but I've still got a case or two going, some stuff I can look into while I'm out here. I owe it to Phil to get something done since he was generous enough to turn his head for me on this thing."

"Oh. Well then. You're working. You're fine."

"I'm fine," David agreed with a laugh. Sascha thought that the Bureau was life itself and, for the most part, so did he. It was just another reason the two of them got along so well.

"I'm fine," he repeated for his friend's sake. "You can go back to the beautiful Bridget."

"Bridget. Isn't that a luminous name, David?"

"It's a beautiful name, Sasch," he agreed as they ended their conversation and hung up.

But it wasn't the name "Bridget" that was on his mind as he glanced out the window later and watched the moon climb through the sky. There was another lady on his mind, and try as hard as he could, he couldn't get her out of his thoughts.

* * *

Gretchen was trudging down the street with Goliath, the heavy leaves of the trees dripping shadows onto the sidewalk glowing in the moonlight. It had been a long day and the extra paperwork involved in arresting Wayne had made the day even longer. Not that she regretted the arrest. Peggy might not be able to pull away from the man she'd married and who abused her, but at least she would know that there were people who cared, that if she ever did feel she could make the break, there would be those who would help her.

The thought conjured up a sudden vision of intense green eyes. David had taken Peggy under his wing as if she were a wounded child. He had treated his mother with warmth and solicitousness when she had arrived. And he had insisted on driving when he'd known she was still reacting to the inevitable fatigue that followed the keyed-up moments detectives faced as a part of their daily regimen. He was the kind of man who looked for signs of need in a woman and he responded to those needs. He took care of people, was most likely used to having women falling all over him and relying on him. It was probably what had helped make him as an agent, that urge to make a difference. And yet, his very warmth was what made him dangerous to her, especially when she was tired. It would be so easy to press close into that warmth and snuggle close.

"Not the right thing to do, Neal," she whispered, catching Goliath's attention and smiling at him to urge him onward. When she dated, she always dated men out of her field, men who had barriers as high as her own. A little fun was all she wanted from a man. Not warmth, not someone who responded to her needs. That meant ties, sticky connections, the danger of getting in and not being able to get out, and she always made sure she knew where the door was when she went into a room or into a relationship. No way did she ever want to become the kind of woman who would trail a man around the country and give up most of the things she held dear. That had been her mother, and her mother had been an old and used-up woman long before physical age had taken its toll. That life wasn't for her. The single life held way too many charms and benefits to ever give it up.

That thought was sailing through her head as she neared a small blue cottage and Goliath began pulling on his leash. He barked softly, then whimpered when Gretchen ordered him to be quiet.

"I know," she said sympathetically. "That little Pomeranian with the twitchy tail lives here, doesn't she? But we've got to be careful, Goliath, you and I. Your lady love has an owner who's very particular about whom her pet associates with. It isn't easy, this relationship stuff, is it? Even if you just want to keep things easy and light, things have a nasty way of mixing themselves up. Let's go home, shall we?"

And so they turned toward the home that Gretchen still loved knowing was hers alone. A sense of warmth, of letting go and giving in to the sleepiness that had been waiting at the backs of her eyes for hours kicked in, and Gretchen knew why. She was heading back to her sanctuary. She'd picked out every stick of furniture in her tiny neat house, she hadn't had to make concessions for anyone. There she could do whatever she wanted, say whatever she wanted, live just as she and she alone wanted. It was her idea of heaven, her house, and they were almost back to heaven when she and Goliath ran into David.

Looking up into his dark smiling eyes, she should have been irritated at having her plans interrupted.

Gretchen smiled back. "Lost, rich boy?"

His chuckle slid in and caressed her senses in the most dangerous of ways.

He slowly shook his head.

"Not nearly lost," he confessed. "I saw Goliath's white coat bobbing down the street and I thought I'd stop and say hi," he said, bending to greet the dog.

"Hi," she said. "But what are you doing so far from home this late, David? Were you at the office working?"

"For a while. Mostly, though, I thought I'd come fill you in on Peggy's progress. I know how you feel about this town and being the caretaker of the inhabitants here. My mother's made Peggy an offer. Help finding a job to get her on her feet and independent and in the meanwhile, room and board and all the time she needs to think her life through. A chance to be away from Wayne for a bit and get her world together in a safe environment if she wants it. Peg's considering it."

He fell into step beside her as they rounded the corner and headed up the walkway to her place. "I'm glad," she said, and her voice floated softly on the whisper of a breeze that lifted the pale tendrils of her hair, a breeze that smelled of summertime grass recently clipped and flowers. "Would you like to come in?" she asked, wondering where those oh so dangerous words had come from.

He gazed down at her. His eyes darkened, narrowed. "Yes." The word came out harsh and fierce. As if he realized that, he folded his hands into fists, took a deep breath and backed off half an inch. "But I probably shouldn't."

He was right. He shouldn't. But he had brought her this news that she was happy to hear. He'd brought it because he knew she'd want to hear it, Gretchen told herself, and for no other reason. So…how could she be less of a good neighbor?

"I'll make a pot of decaf," she said.

"You'll put your feet up and enjoy a few minutes with Goliath. I'm the intruder. I'll make the coffee."

Gretchen smiled. "I thought I was the bossy one."

"You are. Don't let anyone tell you differently."

"Of course I won't. Bossy people generally don't let anyone tell them anything they don't want them to." And as they walked in the door, she unleashed Goliath, washed her hands and went straight to the coffeepot.

David chuckled. "Making a point?"

She was. Men had tried to take the reins from her before. And they'd failed. It was part of the reason why she didn't want to marry. She was too used to going her own way, too used to being the one in charge. She liked being the strong one.

But as David came up behind her and rested his hands on her shoulders, as the warmth of his hands and his body and the soap and aftershave and male scent of him drifted around her, Gretchen couldn't keep her hands from jostling slightly, the water sloshing just a bit.

"David," she drawled in warning.

"Shh," he whispered, bending his head, his breath warm at her ear. "You've had a long day and you've had your way, haven't you? You're making the coffee, aren't you?"

His long, lean fingers kneaded her skin, gently stroking, soothing, sliding over her. The tension of fatigue fled, the tension of being touched by a man who knew just how to turn her nerves to fire grew.

"What…what are you doing?" She barely got the words past her suddenly dry lips.

"Relaxing you. I realize now that I shouldn't have come over here. You're tired and now you're making me coffee."

"You brought me news I wanted to hear."

His fingers slid beneath the thin cotton of her blouse. His skin met hers. Gretchen closed her eyes. She carefully lowered the coffeepot to the counter.

"David?"

He nudged aside thick strands of her hair, placing his lips against the side of her neck, and she sagged against him.

Somehow she turned in his arms. She looked up into those hot green eyes.

"I—" She parted her lips, snagging his attention.

"Tomorrow. We'll worry about the reasons why not tomorrow," he promised as he caught his hands around her narrow waist and pulled her high and tight against him. "For now…this."

His lips covered her own as he claimed her. Hard, hungry lips that molded to the softness of her mouth, then gentled as he nibbled at her.

David pulled back slightly and she followed him. Gretchen raised her hands, gripped his shirt and found his lips again.

His hands skimmed her waist, climbed her back. He slid his fingers over her sensitive skin, bringing them forward to cup her breasts.

A low moan curled deep in her throat, barely escaping. She leaned closer still.

"Gretchen." The word came out on a groan, just as Goliath barked.

The sudden, unexpected sound sent Gretchen pushing back from David. Her breathing was labored, and David's eyes looked dazed, still cloudy with desire.

Her own probably did, too. She looked away, down at her little dog.

"It's all right, Goliath," she managed to say, knowing that it was not all right at all. She had been kissing David, practically tearing his shirt from him. His hands had been everywhere, delighting her, seducing her. She shouldn't have been enjoying this time with this man in this way. Besides, it was late and both of them had work tomorrow. They had to work together—as partners solving a crime, not as lovers.

She kept her eyes on her dog, collecting her thoughts, enforcing a calm on herself she didn't truly feel. But Goliath wasn't looking at her or even at David. He was dancing in front of the window.

David gave her one last intense look and moved to the window. He was probably making sure she was all right, Gretchen guessed, making sure Goliath hadn't scared away an intruder. The darn man just had way too much protective male in him.

"He probably just saw an owl," Gretchen said. "Goliath's a little high strung."

"You should keep this down at night," David said, pulling down the shade.

"Yes. I should. I usually do, but—"

"But tonight your partner interfered and caught you by surprise."

It was the truth. She hadn't been acting very smart from the moment David had shown up.

She bit her lip.

"Don't do that," he said. "Don't start getting that I-shouldn't-have-been-kissing-a-fellow-officer look."

Somehow she dredged up a smile. "Well?"

"*I* shouldn't have started it," he said, taking the blame. "It was definitely my doing. But you know what, Gretchen?" David moved to the door, a slow smile on his lips.

"What?"

"I don't regret kissing you. Not one bit."

He paused, his hand cupping the doorknob as he looked back over his shoulder. "And I think I should give you fair warning. Someday I'm going to kiss you again when I get the chance. But not tonight."

She raised one brow. "Not in the mood anymore, David?"

He chuckled at that. "Very much in the mood, Gretchen. Which is exactly why I'm leaving. You're tired tonight, and I have the feeling we're both going to need every ounce of energy we can muster when we finally make love."

And with that, he pulled the door open and stepped outside.

Gretchen blinked twice as the door snapped shut behind him. She told herself to breathe.

The man was totally outrageous. But then, she'd known that. What other kind of agent would come in and ask to take part in an investigation he had absolutely no right to be on? What kind of man was David Hannon, after all?

"A very sexy one, Goliath. A man who makes my

fingers itch, my toes curl, and every part of my body ache. And that makes him dangerous. No way am I letting my guard down around David Hannon again. I probably shouldn't invite him into my house again, either. And don't go giving me that look. The man is trouble. Big trouble, and we're not looking for trouble, are we?"

Goliath gave a short bark.

But, Gretchen wondered, did that bark mean yes or no?

Celeste Monroe stared blankly out her window of the Big Sky Bed & Breakfast. The night was warm but slightly breezy. That should have made it pleasant, good sleeping weather, but there was no way she could sleep, Celeste knew, turning to pace up and down the deep carpeting of her room. The dreams were chasing her again.

Something was wrong with this case regarding Raven Hunter. Something really bad. Something she should remember. Why couldn't she remember any of it?

Every time she thought of Raven or Jeremiah, she felt fear. Cold droplets of sweat trickled down her back, dampening her nightgown. Nausea rose up within her.

There were so many questions rattling through her head. How could she sleep?

She knew that Jeremiah was being blamed for Raven's death. Something wasn't right with that. If she could only remember what it was, if she could fill in the blank spots, dredge up the parts of that long-ago nightmarish night that eluded her.

She didn't know what had happened, but she knew one thing. She loved her nephew desperately and she didn't want him digging into this case. Nothing good could come of that.

If only she could remember why. If only she knew why her sister Blanche had come to her in those restless dreams she'd had. *A day of spiritual awakening,* Blanche had said. Soon she would have an awakening.

The only question was, Did she really want to have an awakening? Which was worse, the truth or the night-mares? And what if David discovered the truth and it was as bad as she feared?

What if what he discovered was unchangeable, un-forgivable, as awful as the constant tremors running through her led her to believe?

Dark pain and anguish filled her soul. Regret. Fear. So much to lose. So much to flee from. She'd been fleeing for a long time.

Only now there was news. Evidence of sorts. Some-thing that might jar the memory and let everything come flowing back to her somehow. And now David had come home to find out the truth.

She loved him. He was her nephew and she loved him almost as much as she loved her own children. Fondly. Ferociously. She would sacrifice her own safety for his, she loved him that much. But none of that mattered, because she didn't want him here. Not like this.

Somehow she had to find the answers he was seeking before he did. If she did that, maybe she could be ready. She'd go to the station. Maybe that would help her remember. And maybe she could finally find some peace and some rest.

Five

"You didn't have to climb the tree to get the cat, David. This isn't the sixteenth century. We have machinery that lifts us right up into the branches. Amazing stuff."

David heard the curt tone in Gretchen's voice and couldn't help smiling.

"Worried about me, Gretch?"

She let out her breath in a whoosh as they finally made it back to her office. She'd been silent all the way back to town. Now her eyes were flashing green sparks when she turned to him.

"Yes, David. Of course I'm angry. Weren't you the one who just a week ago said that you were now responsible for my life and I was responsible for yours? How do you think I would feel if you fell out of that tree and killed yourself?"

"I don't have to ask. I know, Gretchen, that you would feel you were somehow to blame."

She stood there looking up at him silently with those light green eyes of hers and he wanted to take her in his arms and tell her not to worry. He wanted to crush her softness beneath his hardness, to wrap her up in white sheets and roll with her in a big bed. He wanted to chase those shadows from her eyes.

"You could have fallen," she reiterated.

"It wasn't that far, Gretchen," he said gently. "I've climbed much higher, been in a thousand times more danger." It hadn't been that high, although she was probably right. It would have been much simpler and easier to wait for the right equipment, but the child on the ground had been worried, and even Gretchen had looked a bit concerned about the tiny gray kitten up in the tree. And besides, darn it, he'd just needed some activity, anything to chase away the restlessness that had been edging into him lately. His hands were tied on this case. His hands were also tied where touching Gretchen was concerned, it seemed. Because the lady just wasn't at all certain that she wanted his hands on her soft body. And he'd been thinking of nothing all day but that kiss they'd shared last night. He wanted his hands and his lips on her very badly.

She blinked suddenly, as if reading his thoughts, and then finally shook her head. "All right, it wasn't that high," she agreed. "And I'm sorry for complaining. I'm just…a bit tense this morning. I wanted to talk to you. Last night—what happened last night—it shouldn't have. It can't. Not again. You have to know that as well as I do."

He reached out. She backed away a step. "I mean it, Hannon. You're my assistant."

"A temporary one," he told her. "And I don't, in reality, work for you at all. I'm FBI. You're one of

Whitehorn's finest. And very fine at that. Exquisite, in fact."

"David."

Her lips mouthed the words just as another voice said the same word behind them.

Both Gretchen and David turned to see his aunt standing in the doorway. Celeste was clutching a large hemp bag, her fingers wrapped around the tortoiseshell handle. Her long rust skirt with the tan leaves besprinkled in the folds flowed out around her as she rocked back and forth on her heels.

"Well, David, here you are," she said briskly in that no-nonsense tone she'd always used to hide the very soft person dwelling inside. "I just…well, since I was in town, I thought I'd pop in for a minute to see you and make sure you were taking care of yourself. Your schedule's so erratic these days, I thought it would be nice to just say hello. Besides, your mother wanted to check and see if you would be home for dinner tonight."

"Aunt Celeste," he said, stepping forward and folding her into his arms. "What a nice surprise. You know Gretchen, of course."

"Celeste," Gretchen said, holding out her hand.

"Well, of course I know Gretchen," Celeste agreed. "She's been out to Big Sky to question me. I understand she's extremely good at her job. I have no doubt at all that the two of you will be finding who's responsible for all the upheaval in the town. Do you think you'll find the person soon? Are you close?"

She opened her eyes wider and glanced at both her nephew and Gretchen.

"It's an old case. Could take time," David said, smiling at his aunt. "Come in. Sit down and rest."

"No, no, that's fine. I'll just be in and out. So you still don't know what happened? You don't really think it was Jeremiah, do you, David?" She let go of her purse with one hand and grasped a bunch of her skirt, twisting the fabric in her fingers.

"Mrs. Monroe," Gretchen began gently, "I know this must be difficult for you, but truly this case is still open. We can't make assumptions."

"Come on, Aunt Celeste," David said, taking her by the elbow. "Let me give you a lift home." He glanced over his shoulder at Gretchen and she nodded back at him as he gently led his aunt out of the office.

"I'm—really, I'm fine, David," Celeste said as they made it to the sidewalk. "I just wondered. That was all. And, anyway, I do have my car here. Will you be home for dinner?"

"I promise we'll all be together tonight, Celeste. I'll even dress for dinner and come prepared to entertain mother's guests. Maybe I'll even bring a guest." He nodded pointedly toward the building they'd just vacated.

Celeste's dark eyes softened just a bit. "That would be nice, David. She's very pretty, isn't she?"

"She's lovely *and* accomplished, too, Aunt Celeste."

"Well, of course she is. Rafe told me so himself when I saw him right after he put her in charge of this investigation. Besides, your mother will approve."

David leaned back and looked his aunt straight in the eye.

"Well, we never get to meet the women you're involved with," she said.

He chuckled at that. "Don't use the word 'involved' in front of Gretchen. I'm afraid she'll walk out the door."

"Well, of course. You're her…"

"I believe the word you're looking for is 'partner,' Aunt Celeste. As in business associate."

"Partner, yes."

"Yes, exactly," he said to himself as she walked away. Partner. He'd better remember the word if he didn't want Gretchen to run.

"You've invited me to dinner at the Big Sky?" Gretchen asked a few minutes later.

David grinned. "At the Big Sky. And don't look so suspicious. We're just going to feed you. I can guarantee that I won't try slipping you into bed under the watchful eyes of my mother. Not that she'd object."

Gretchen's eyes opened wide. "You've done that before?"

His grin gave way to low, sexy laughter. "No, and that's why she wouldn't object. My mother would assume that if I was serious enough about a woman that I would risk sneaking her into a guest bedroom when there are so many other more obviously private places, that I would be making a more or less public declaration of my intentions."

"Your intentions being…"

"Taking a wife, making babies, shooting for forever."

Gretchen drank in a long breath of air. "I see."

"Yes, I guess you do. So we're just talking dinner tonight. We'll save our private moments for a private place."

"David?"

He looked down at her, giving her his full attention.

"Has any woman ever told you that you are absolutely shameless?"

"Yes, I believe they have. A few teachers. My aunt. My mother."

"Not the women you date?"

He shrugged. "I wouldn't call most of what I do dating. In my line of work I do a lot of things…on the run, so to speak."

The slightest pink glow settled on her cheeks. As if she'd felt the heat, Gretchen rubbed one hand over her jaw, then slipped it into her pocket, suddenly standing up straighter.

"So there'll be no settling down for you, either?" she asked.

"I'm a bit of a loner. Always have been."

She stared at him for several silent seconds, her lips soft, her eyes even softer—maybe even a tad worried—before she nodded.

"Then I suppose there's no problem with us having dinner," she conceded. "This will simply be a visit between colleagues."

His smile was rueful.

"What?" she asked.

"You were way too happy to find out that I live my life on the solitary side," he pointed out.

She shrugged one shoulder. "Well, it just makes things easier knowing that you don't get involved. You already know that I don't. Not that being a loner is an essential part of my nature. I have a world of friends and relations so there's always company when I want some, and I want that company frequently, but I choose to *live* alone. So, yes, it's nice to know that we see eye-to-eye on this issue, and, yes, dinner with your family will be lovely. I've missed seeing them. I suppose being involved in this investigation has made me pull back just a bit. In a town this size, the professional and personal often overlap and sometimes I walk a fine line. You don't think anyone will feel uncomfortable having me there, given the circumstances?"

"Well, if they do, then I suppose they'd feel uncomfortable having me there, too. We're in this case together, Gretchen. And besides, my family understands that this case isn't about you or me. It's about justice. My parents instilled the need for justice in me at an early age. I suppose that's part of the reason I elected to get involved in the type of work I'm in."

"Your parents have always struck me as very fair people," she agreed. "Do you think Frannie and Austin will be there? I haven't seen your sister much lately. I like her."

Her voice sounded so eager, he couldn't help holding out one hand as if he wanted to capture that eagerness, brush his fingers over the softness of her lips in a long, slow caress.

He caught himself just in time.

"Sorry, partner," he said, lowering his hand to his side again. "I'll try to behave in public tonight, and I'll make a point of calling Frannie. Cleo, too. We'll make it a special occasion."

"The traveler finally comes home to the heart of his family?"

"And he brings a date," he said with a wicked grin.

She raised her brows. "Is that what I am?"

"No, but I thought I'd gone too long without getting a rise out of you."

She chuckled. "I'm wise to you, Hannon. I'm learning how you think. You're going to find it harder and harder to get a reaction from me."

But as she pulled back to walk away from him, he did raise his hand. He let his fingers trail down her cheek. And then he bent and placed his lips just where his fingers had been.

"Tonight," he promised her. And though he'd meant to prove something to her, that he could indeed get a reaction from her—and judging by the dusky pink of skin, he definitely had—the jolt of pure desire that skimmed through him proved something even more to himself. His reaction to Gretchen Neal was getting stronger. He was going to have to either back away or else move forward and move on. There was, after all, no other choice but to sit and simmer and hunger for the lady's touch.

And that was a dangerous combination. A man—or a woman—who was spending all his or her time steeped in desire wasn't thinking about the business at hand. And in his and Gretchen's business, that kind of preoccupation could be deadly.

"David? You there?" David was almost ready to step out the door on his way to pick up Gretchen for the evening when Sascha's call came through.

"Sasch? What's wrong?" Hearing the slur in his friend's voice, David gripped the phone so hard he thought the plastic might bend.

"What could be wrong, my friend? I'm fine, very fine. It's you I'm worried about," Sascha said, his voice dipping down low and sad.

"Nothing to worry about here, Sasch," David said quietly. "Everything's fine."

"No. It's not. I heard it in your voice the other day. You're getting tangled up with your Detective Neal."

"We're working together, Sascha. Why are you worried? Have you heard something about Gretchen that I should know?"

Sascha's laugh was low and harsh. "Who needs to hear anything? She's a woman, isn't she?"

Ah, so now they were getting to the point. "Sascha, has something happened between you and Bridget?"

Silence. Complete and utter silence.

"Sasch? Answer me."

More silence, then a muffled curse. "What could happen? I told her I wanted to marry her, she decided she loved her ex-husband more. As if I didn't know better. Hell, I've been married, David. I've been up that mountain, and it was an awful, unpredictable and ultimately disappointing climb. Why did I think I wanted to risk that again?"

"I'm so sorry, Sascha. You're sure she's gone for good?"

"She ran like a rabbit caught in the crossfire of two hunters. And what's more, you know Ted Cosgrove?"

"Sure. Nice guy."

"Nice divorced guy. Or almost divorced. His wife left him just last week. She wanted to be free and now Ted can barely see how to tie his shoes in the morning. He looks awful. He feels awful," Sascha said, clearly equipped with firsthand knowledge of what the man was going through.

A long sigh slipped through David. He wanted to take his friend's pain. Damn, he wanted to be there to help Sascha, but that wasn't possible. "Sasch, I wish—"

"Don't wish. I didn't call to talk to you about Bridget or even about Ted, Dave. Not really. I just called to tell you to stay the same as you always have been. Be careful if a woman makes your clothes fit too tight and your head swim and your heart bang around inside your body like an atomic Ping-Pong ball. You know that feeling, David?"

He wasn't sure if he knew that feeling exactly, but he had a pretty good idea what his friend was referring to. And he was also pretty sure Sascha was right. About being careful.

"I won't do anything impetuous, Sascha," he promised.

A low groan followed. "David, your middle name is impetuous."

David felt his smile forming. If his friend could tease him just a little, Sascha's world still held a bit of brightness.

"Yeah, but I have a good friend who keeps the reins on me. Thanks, Sascha," he said.

"No. Thank you," Sascha told him. "I really did call to talk about Bridget, I guess. It's helped to hear your voice."

And it had helped to hear his friend's voice, too, David realized. Sascha had sprinkled in that tinge of reality he'd been grasping for and missing these past few days with Gretchen. Now maybe he could get on with things, with work, and just leave the lady alone, the way she wanted to be left alone.

But first, he was taking her to a family dinner. He had a pretty good feeling that Sascha would have begged him not to do this.

It wouldn't have worked. This far, at least, he was committed.

"But this is where we hit the end of the line, Hannon,"

David reminded himself. "That's the way the lady wants things and the way you have to want them, too."

"It's so very good to see you here, my dear," Edward Hannon was saying just a short time later, taking Gretchen's hand in his own. "You don't need to be a stranger, does she, Yvette?"

Yvette smiled and let out a low laugh. "As if you and I had ever met a stranger, Edward. But you know what he means, don't you, Gretchen? Or maybe you don't. Edward and I tend to follow a different drummer, as they say. I think we may have been a sore trial to our straitlaced little Frannie."

Little Frannie, a grown and very married woman, smiled and pressed a kiss to her mother's cheek. "And you know I love you for being just who you are."

"Yes, but I sometimes think you felt a bit uncomfortable. Perhaps you would have liked a few more rules. Perhaps you should have had them if you needed them. Anyway, Gretchen, dear, please don't be a stranger anymore. We like seeing you. We're glad to have you here tonight. You did well, David," she said, as if he'd just gotten an A on his report card.

He gave his mother a lazy, indulgent smile and Gretchen suspected he was used to his mother praising him as if he were still unable to tie his shoes without help.

"David climbed a tree yesterday to retrieve a lost kitten. He didn't even wait for the cherry picker to come," she volunteered before she realized just how juvenile her own words sounded.

"Of course," Edward said. "He wouldn't. David always did do things his own way. We worried about him a bit as a child, but really, there wasn't any reason to worry. David was just David. Rules never seemed to apply to him."

"Yes, he broke every one and somehow managed to get away with it, too," Frannie said with a laugh. "I was always in awe of how he did it. But I suppose you're a bit of a rule breaker, too, Gretchen. It takes a rather adventurous sort to go into law enforcement."

"Maybe," Gretchen agreed. "For me it was just a natural progression. I'd grown up taking care of all my brothers and sisters, helping them fight their battles and making sure their rights weren't violated. I fell in love with law enforcement right from the start."

"I hear you got Wayne Sadine to go for counseling and to try joining AA," Cleo said. "That's quite an accomplishment. Wayne was always pigheaded."

Gretchen shrugged. "I think his willingness to try had more to do with the fact that the powerful Hannons have taken Peggy under their wings. For the first time someone gave him a reason to want to change. How is Peggy, by the way?"

"She's a delight," Yvette said. "I feel so very sorry that I never thought to interfere enough to offer to take her in."

But David had. His first thought had been to get Peggy out of harm's way.

"Don't worry, my dear," Edward said. "She'll have a place here for as long as she wishes. And it won't be charity, either. She's a bright young lady, one who insists on pitching in to help out in whatever way she can. If she wants a job here, there's always plenty to do. If not, we'll help her find work elsewhere and get back on her feet. She won't have to be dependent on a man if she doesn't want to be."

His kind stare told her that he understood that not being dependent was an important issue for her. She smiled her gratitude.

"Why don't you take Gretchen for a tour of the Big Sky, David?" he offered. "I'm not sure she's ever seen the place by moonlight."

"Yes, Gretchen, it's really quite beautiful at night," Celeste said.

"Rather romantic," Yvette agreed.

"How could I turn down such a lovely offer?" Gretchen asked, rising from the table. The black silk of her short dress swished against the tablecloth as David slid her chair back and held out his hand.

"My family's pretty smooth, aren't they?" he asked with a twinkle in his eye as they moved out onto the moonlit terrace. "I'm sure they think I was being a bit slow about luring you out here."

Gretchen couldn't help laughing as she looked up into his dark eyes. The man was sinfully handsome in formal black and white. And she knew from experience that there wasn't anything the slightest bit slow about him.

"I think your family is delightful. Your parents move together as if they're a single unit. It's obvious that they adore each other. I can see why the Big Sky attracts so many people to come here and then to come back again. Who could resist such a warm, caring atmosphere?"

"Ah, then, you're saying that you find us irresistible, are you, Ms. Neal? In that case, let me pull you farther into the shadows."

He slid his hand up her bare arm to the naked skin of her back. "Mmm, you should dress this way around the office," he told her.

"It's not very practical," she said suddenly. "I wasn't quite sure what to wear for a meal at the Big Sky."

"Anything," he told her. "Denim. Silk. Nothing. But this is nice. Very nice."

"David," she said, placing her hand on his chest as he leaned closer. "Your family—they don't think—"

"That we're lovers? I'm not privy to their thoughts, Gretchen."

"But you know them so well."

Yes, he did, and he knew that his parents, liberal as they were, would like him to settle down closer to home.

"You're not in danger with me, Gretchen. I promise you that."

"I wasn't afraid of that. You don't frighten me, David."

"What does frighten you? Anything?"

She studied his question for long minutes. "Commitment. Boredom. Being tied to someone so that their life has too great an effect on mine. That was my mother. Always following my father around. Always raising babies. And because I was the oldest, it was my life, too. I don't want that, David."

He rested his forehead on hers, looked down into her moonlit, worried eyes. "Then you're safe, Gretchen. In spite of my warm, loving family, they were very busy people when I was growing up, and I was a somewhat sickly kid. I didn't fit in with other kids and I learned to like my own company, my own way of doing things. After years of forging a solitary path, I'm not a good candidate for marriage, I'm afraid. You've seen how pigheaded and stubborn and pushy I can be. I'm not likely to change or to want to change. So you're safe from me in that sense."

"In that sense?"

He nodded, grazing her jaw with his lips. "But not any other. Because I *am* pushy and pigheaded and stubborn, Gretchen. That said, I'd still leave you alone if you weren't attracted to me. You're not attracted?"

"I'm not blind to your charms, Hannon. I'm a woman, after all."

His lips rose in a smile against the bare skin of her throat and he kissed his way up to her lips. He touched his mouth to hers, then pulled away just a breath.

"And I'm a man, Gretchen. Neither of us may want marriage, but I want you in every other way a man can want a woman."

"And you're a stubborn man, I've heard. Someone seems to have told me that."

"I wonder who," he said, kissing her again.

"Some silly man, no doubt. Should we go back inside?" she asked, her head falling back as he found the soft curve of her breast with his teeth and nipped slightly.

"No."

"No," she agreed.

And he slid his hands up her body and placed a chaste kiss on the top of her head.

"No?" she asked.

"Not yet. Not until we have a proper bed and not until we're away from a roomful of people speculating on what we're doing."

"Mmm, they might make me marry you if I ravished you," she agreed.

"Indeed," he agreed. "My family looks out for those who try to take advantage of other people."

"I want to take advantage of you, David."

He slid his arm along hers and found her hand. "I

know. And the fact that you've said that leads me to the truth."

"The truth? As in, who killed Raven Hunter?"

"Exactly. And, also, who filled Gretchen Neal's wineglass one too many times?"

She stared up at him. "I'm not drunk, David."

"No, but you're happy enough to lose all those prickly inhibitions that usually inhabit your body. When I have you—and I mean to—I want you inhibitions and all."

"I see," she said, leaning close to kiss him on the shoulder right through the black linen of his suit. "I wonder who did fill up my wineglass too many times."

He groaned low in his throat and led her to his car. "The same fool who's going to drive you home right now. The man who doesn't intend to make that same mistake again."

"The next time will be different? Will there be a next time?"

"I guarantee there'll be a next time, Gretchen. And maybe even a next and a next. I have the feeling that you and I are going to need a few 'next times' to get each other out of our systems."

She leaned back against the seat as he handed her into the car and fastened her seat belt against her hips.

"I'd like that, David. To get you out of my system. It's very difficult getting my job done when I'm always looking up into your eyes."

"Gretchen?"

"Yes?" Her voice was dreamy and soft and sleepy.

"Don't say another word," he said as he joined her in the car. "And just be grateful that my family instilled in me a certain amount of fortitude. It's that and only that that's saving us both from behaving very foolishly tonight."

But when he looked over, he found that Gretchen had gone limp with sleep. He lifted her hand and kissed her slender fingers before starting the car.

"Let's get you home, partner. Tomorrow you have to be tough and in charge again. Tomorrow we take things a step further."

Six

Gretchen held the sea-green breath of a dress up in front of her the next day. Except for the jacket, meant to be worn during the church service for Pamela's wedding, the gown was simplicity itself. With spaghetti straps and a neckline that dipped in a simple low scoop, the pale clingy material hugged the body in a long straight line to the floor.

"No wonder Pamela wanted to make sure it fit," Gretchen said to a curious Goliath as she slipped into the gown one more time just to make sure. "One extra spoonful of chocolate ice cream could mean disaster with a gown like this." As it was, the dress smoothed over her curves like a caress. It was perfect, except… she looked like a woman in search of a man.

"Which only means one thing, Goliath. My family will be on the prowl, out scouring the streets and parking lots looking for a man for me. They'll consider this dress a slap in the face, a reminder that once again I'm all dressed up without a proper husband to take me home and impregnate me. And then they'll start looking for a husband for me. Again."

She must have said that last word just a little too firmly. There must have been just a bit too much tension in her voice, because Goliath tilted his head and backed away a step or two.

She chuckled softly. "Don't worry, Goliath. I'm not mad at all males. I just don't see why everyone thinks I absolutely must have one to take home and keep forever. And you know, there's only one way to fight the inevitable, don't you? I'll just have to keep dancing all night. A different man for every song. Otherwise, my best friends and family are going to do their darnedest to pick out a suitable mate to claim my time and my attention. The evening will be long and slow and painful."

A short, sharp bark signaled her doggy buddy's agreement.

"You know what I mean, don't you, Goliath? I know how you like to play the field. The truth is that someday, somehow, I'm just going to have to make the truth clear to them. I'm not a marrying kind of woman. And that's final. When I wear this dress, I'm going to have the time of my life, and I'm going to go home alone at the end of the night."

It appeared that Jackson Hawk had finally located Storm, but there was still a question mark as to when the man was going to show up. That fact didn't sit well with David. Another day had passed, they were no closer to a break, and he wanted this case solved. His aunt was clearly being affected much too much by all the upheaval, and he himself couldn't stay away from his work too long. Phil had been indulgent and understanding about his need to—finally—take some time for himself, but his time, after all, belonged to the government, something Gretchen had been asking him about just that morning. Trying to get rid of him more quickly, David suspected with a frown.

"He did say that he was coming in for questioning, though, didn't he?" David had prompted.

Jackson had sighed. "Storm's always been a very private person," he'd admitted. "He's not exactly one for allowing himself to be pinned down easily or for declaring himself, but—"

"But?" Gretchen had coaxed.

"I can guarantee that he'll be here—and that he'll be angry when he arrives," Jackson had promised.

Her shrug had been resigned. "It's to be expected," she'd said.

But after Jackson had gone, David hadn't missed the worried look in her eyes. "You're worried about Storm?"

She shook her head. "He's a man who lost his brother many years ago. And now he's had to face that loss all over again. The families are always angry. Why shouldn't they be?"

And David knew just how much this lady had gone through back on those streets of Miami. She'd seen more than her share of the tough stuff.

"Whitehorn shouldn't be this way," he said, wishing they were in a more private place than the station so he could risk placing a soothing arm around her shoulder or even pulling her in close against his side, dropping a kiss on the flowery fragrance of her silky hair.

She surprised him with the small smile that turned her light green eyes bright. "It usually isn't this way," she promised. "Your hometown is a wonderful place, David. Don't think it isn't just because a few bad things happen now and then. And don't go getting that let's-take-care-of-Gretchen light in your eyes. I'm a very resilient individual."

"A woman who handles things."

She shrugged. "Aren't you a man who handles things? Whatever led you into the Bureau in the first place?"

He laughed out loud at that. "Stubbornness, I'm sure my family would tell you. I was a puny, sickly kid and when I hit college and started bulking up, I was determined to prove that I could play hardball. Purely pig-headed."

"Hmm. I can believe that, but I doubt that was the only reason you went into your line of work. Plenty of other opportunities elsewhere to prove yourself. Admit it, Hannon, you're a sucker for truth and justice. You like to make sure that the good guys win."

She stood in front of him, her hands firmly planted on her hips, her chin thrust out in challenge. An immovable wall, sure that she was right.

He lifted one shoulder. "I like to even the odds," he admitted. "I like to make sure things are done fairly."

Gretchen noted that David, who smiled so wickedly and so well, wasn't smiling now. She guessed that he'd seen his share of injustice as a kid. If he'd truly been scrawny and sickly as he'd said, she could well imagine what he'd had to put up with, even if he did have the Hannon name behind him. Maybe *because* he bore the Hannon name. He would have been a target now and then. But no more. He'd grown up. He'd grown gorgeous and tall and strong. He'd found his place, his self-confidence, and he attracted people, especially women, like roses attracted helpless bumblebees. He did it with that sense of justice, that humor, those eyes, and that wicked, wicked smile that promised pleasure beyond belief.

She was no different. She was susceptible. The temptation to rise up on her toes and feel those lips against hers again was almost overwhelming. And that was why she'd spent the morning drowning in paperwork. If there was anything destined to drown out desire, it was paperwork.

"Gretchen—Officer Neal, do you think you could do something about my next door neighbor? I mean, I don't want you to arrest him or hit him with your club or anything. Not yet, anyway. I just want you to kind of shake him up a little bit."

Uh-oh. Here we go again, David thought, raising one brow as Gretchen slowed to let the spindly man walking behind her have time to catch up. She steered him toward the sensible, neighborly way to handle his sticky problem of his neighbor cutting across his yard on his way to work. This kind of question-and-answer session seemed to follow the lady like shadows trailing sunlight. In the past week and a half since he'd become Gretchen's almost constant companion, David had come to realize that while the lady was fully competent in her role as law enforcer, she spent a substantial amount of her time soothing and mothering the citizens of the town who depended on her.

They'd almost made it all the way to the Hip Hop

Café, David noted. Lunch was only a few steps away, and Gretchen very much needed her lunch. First thing this morning there'd been the news from Jackson, which had been less than they'd hoped for. And then she'd spent the rest of the morning wrestling with paperwork, which he knew she hated. Heck, everyone in law enforcement hated paperwork and there only seemed to be more and more of it as the years went on. So it had been a crummy morning. A draining morning. A give-me-sustenance kind of morning. Did the lady really need any more of this nonsense?

No, she didn't, but David was absolutely, completely positive she wouldn't appreciate him butting into her business, either. And so he settled for giving the man disgruntled looks.

When she'd finally soothed Harve's nerves and joined David, walking beside him into the café, she lightly nudged him in the ribs with her elbow.

"You weren't very subtle," she said. "You were all but growling. Poor Harve probably thinks the feds are going to raid his house at midnight just because he asked for a little help."

David raised his brows. "He didn't ask for a little help. He asked you to act like his mother, to act as a mediator between his neighbor and him. A grown man like that, he should be ashamed throwing his petty problems off on you."

He lightly touched the small of her back, motioning her toward a booth in the rear.

"They're my problems, too," she insisted.

David snorted. "You can't baby the whole world, lady."

Gretchen stopped in her tracks. She turned and

looked right up into his eyes. Close. She was very close. Near enough for him to catch her to him, to slide his palms around her waist. The thought sent his blood sizzling through his veins.

"I don't baby them, Hannon."

The defensiveness of her tone told him all he wanted to know. She *did* baby the citizens of this town and she darn well knew it. She just didn't want to admit it.

David grinned. "All right, Gretchen, you don't go above and beyond the call of duty. Ever. You're tough as hardtack, cool as ice cream."

Finally, she looked up from beneath her lashes and smiled at him as he urged her to sit in the booth they were standing next to.

She sat. She played with the saltshaker, rolling it between her palms.

"Okay, I do have a tiny tendency to be just a tad proprietary with the people of Whitehorn. I like them to feel that they can talk to me about anything that's bothering them."

"Nothing wrong with that, Gretchen," David said, leaning close. "Except—"

That warning light switched on in her eyes. It occurred to David that he was playing her along in the very hope of seeing that hot green light, that fire that shot through her and right into him.

"Except?" she coaxed.

"Except when people take advantage of your willingness to listen. Except when they become so dependent on you that they don't tend to their own backyards themselves. Except when you don't seem to be able to say no."

Gretchen leaned in close, her face mere inches

from David's. "Are you implying that I'm a bit spineless, David?"

Her voice was a dangerous, low whisper. He loved it, longed to lean forward those few inches and cover her lips with his own, drink in those low, seductive syllables that rolled off her tongue and engage in a sensual battle of tongues and teeth and will. He wanted to absorb the lady right into his skin.

Instead, he took a slow, unsteady breath. He held out his palms in surrender. "Any man who called you spineless would have to be blind, sweetheart."

She looked quickly around the room. To see if anyone had heard the endearment, he was sure.

"Sorry," he said, but of course he wasn't sorry at all and both of them knew it.

"All right, then," she agreed, pulling back, picking up her menu and appearing to study it.

"I could say no," she said quietly, as if she had just told him that she was going to order the meat loaf special.

He chuckled and picked up his own menu. "Bet you couldn't. Not in this lifetime, Gretchen."

"I could." She sat up straighter and fiddled with the plain gold band of her watch. "Tell him, Em."

Emma Harper stood beside the table, ready to take their order. "Tell him what, Gretchen?"

"That I'm not a total pushover when someone asks for my help with their…their community problems."

David smiled up at Emma. "Harve Dibbons wants her to help him with his neighbor who keeps cutting across his lawn."

Emma's light laughter lit up her eyes.

"Oh, that. Sure, Gretchen, face it. You're a pushover.

That is, I'll bet you steered him in the right direction, but you listened to him tell the whole long, drawn-out story first, didn't you?"

Gretchen opened her mouth, her green eyes irritated. "Okay, maybe at times I let people go on, but that's my choice. I could walk away if I wanted to."

"The way you could say no to all those requests to stand up at everyone's wedding?" Emma asked.

"Hey," Gretchen protested. "The world needs its bridesmaids. They keep everyone feeling good, and they take care of the brides of the world. Besides, I only do that for people I'm close to," she insisted.

"You're right. You do, and people ask you because they love you," her friend agreed, and David could hear the sincerity in her voice. "But then they take it too far. Every wedding you stand up at, people are always trying to fix you up with someone when I know you've asked them not to."

Gretchen blew out a breath. She nodded. "I know, and I know they do it because they care, but I am absolutely not looking forward to my part in Pamela's wedding. I adore Pamela, I want to be there, but as for the rest, no, thank you."

But her words and the topic had flipped a switch in David's consciousness.

"I'll bet you can't say no to the next person in town who asks you a foolish question any more than you can turn down one of your friends when they ask you to take part in their weddings."

Gretchen stared him in the eye.

"You're pushing it, Hannon."

"I know. You want to take that bet?"

Gretchen looked up at her friend who was clearly

interested in this topic. A man in the corner was holding up his coffee cup, but Emma was watching Gretchen's lips. Gretchen nodded toward the man and she and David gave the waitress their orders.

"I want to know how this ends," Emma said, her voice a low hiss as she moved away. "You tell me later, Gretchen."

But Gretchen had turned back to David.

"Why would I want to take your bet?"

David slid his palms across the table, his fingertips touching hers. "Because you're a proud, stubborn woman who doesn't want anyone to think that she has an Achilles' heel."

"I don't have one."

He widened his grin, covered her hands with his own. "Well, then?"

"What are the terms?"

He tilted his head. "I win, you invite me to your friend's wedding."

"You don't even know Pamela."

"I know you. And I go with you. We tell everyone I'm your fiancé."

Her eyes widened.

"Why would we do that?"

"So that you can actually enjoy the day. So that you can show everyone you don't need them to find you a man. You don't, of course, but this will simply let everyone relax a bit."

"Except for us."

He shook his head. "Oh, I intend to be very relaxed, Detective Neal, and to enjoy myself. You like to dance?"

She took a deep and visible breath. "Sometimes."

"All right, then."

Gretchen pulled her hands from beneath his. She placed her long, narrow palms over his hands this time. "What happens if I win?"

He studied the room for a moment, tried to think of something that would fly. "I walk your pretend dog for a week."

"Two weeks."

"Done."

She smiled up at him as Emma placed her food in front of her. "Don't think this is going to be an easy bet to win, David," she said.

He grinned at Emma. "What do you think, Emma? A diamond ring or— No, something out of the ordinary. An emerald for her eyes."

Emma shook her head. "What are you talking about, David, you devilish man?"

"Rings, Emma. Rings. Gretchen and I are on the verge of becoming engaged."

"It's not going to happen," Gretchen said.

He reached across the table and brushed her nose with the tip of one finger. "Okay, whatever you say, Gretchen."

"I'm glad you're finally acting more like a true partner," she said with a sarcastic laugh, but her tone was a bit grumpy and uncertain.

It was grumpy and uncertain all day. When he walked her to her car that night, she turned to face him as she put the key in the lock.

"It won't happen, David. Don't look so smug."

He lifted one hand and touched her cheek. "Good night, Detective Neal. Sleep tight."

And he walked away whistling. Who would have

thought that coming to town to solve a murder could have resulted in this much enjoyment?

Lyle Brooks leaned back against the wall of the Whitehorn movie theater and watched David Hannon lean forward and touch Gretchen Neal.

Interesting. His family and Hannon's had never been close, even though they were distantly related. Who would have thought that David would come back to town and snag the attention of his greatest enemy and threat right now? How convenient of the man to do so.

And how interesting that not only were these two working together, they were obviously doing a lot more. They were getting pretty tight.

"Good job, cousin," he muttered. If the two chief investigators were keeping each other company in their spare time, they might be looking the other way now and then. They might be easily distracted, or even better, easily manipulated.

"Oh, I like that," Lyle whispered. "I really do like that. If I need to, I could make use of that little bit of knowledge."

Seven

There were times when a person simply had to admit that she needed a life jacket, Gretchen told herself several days later as she pulled up in the middle of town. This was one of those times. Ever since she'd been thrown together with David Hannon, she'd been struggling to breathe in deep water. The man obviously had way too much experience where women were concerned. She'd seen it that night when she'd had dinner at the Big Sky. He'd been aware of every lady at the table—his sister, his cousins, his aunt, his mother and, oh, yes, herself, as well. He'd been the most gracious of hosts, a man who could make a woman swoon, if women still did that sort of thing.

"But that's not you, Gretchen," she told herself firmly, turning her car off. "You've been courted by men before." And she had. Quite a few men, for that matter. None of them had made a dent in her armor.

So why did she keep finding herself shivering whenever David came into the room?

"Because I'm dealing with a pro, of course," she reminded herself. That was it. Absolutely. The man knew all the right moves, and he had that devilish smile, that long, strong frame, and a look in his eye that made a woman sure that he knew his way around a bedroom way too well.

What's more, ever since they'd made that darn bet, he'd had a lazy, cat-in-the-cream look about him. She was beginning to feel like a very small and tasty mouse whenever David glanced her way.

But not this morning. This morning he'd had calls to make from home. Apparently the government's business didn't stop just because one of their best agents decided to take a few weeks off.

And so she was on her own. She should feel good about that. Back to normal. Free, so to speak.

She should.

"I do," she insisted, slipping through the door of the Hip Hop. This morning for the first time in a while, she'd been on her own. She'd traversed the town alone, made a few calls trying to locate Storm and get him to come in before she had to take stronger measures. And now here she was heading in to lunch all on her own.

"Gretchen?"

The querulous voice came from the first booth, the one she'd just passed.

Gretchen turned to see Lily Mae Wheeler waving her over.

"Gretchen, I just had to see you. That man—o-oh, that man. I just can't even say his name."

Immediately the word "David" appeared in Gretchen's

thoughts. For a second she was almost afraid she'd whispered it out loud.

But apparently she was mistaken. "Him and that darned thick silver hair that covers that equally thick skull," Lily Mae was saying. Her bracelets jangled on her shaking wrist and her beaded earrings swung in fierce opposition as she bobbed her head, trying to force the traitorous name from her lips. "O-oh, that man," Lily Mae said again.

"What man?" Gretchen found her voice long enough to ask the obvious question.

"That man who keeps letting his crabgrass grow over into my yard, that's the one. Do you know what he did yesterday?"

Gretchen was pretty sure she was about to hear.

"Lily Mae..." she began.

But Lily Mae's voice was breaking. "If I had a man living with me, he wouldn't treat me this way. If I weren't alone—"

Immediately Gretchen's heart tipped over. "Lily Mae, I'm sure he doesn't even realize he's upset you. Mr. Vernor is really a very nice man," she said, realizing that Lily Mae was referring to her newest neighbor. "He's kind. If you'd only talk to him."

But the woman was apparently too upset to think about talking to anyone but Gretchen right now. It was a full fifteen minutes before Gretchen could convince the woman that her best course of action was to invite Mr. Vernor over for lemonade and a friendly "chat."

It was well past the time she should have been picking up her menu when she actually did so. She'd barely flipped open the laminated booklet when a shadow fell over her table.

"Hi, sweetheart," David said in that slow, sexy drawl of his. He leaned forward, resting his palms on the table, his lips a breath away from her ear. "How's my sweetest fiancée today?"

She looked up, her eyes wide. She opened her mouth but saw he was nodding toward Lily Mae. "I'm sure you were a help to her, darling Gretchen," he said. "And you've made me the happiest of men."

He took her hand in his own as he sat across from her.

Emma came up, a big smile on her face. "Anything I can do for you two?"

But Gretchen simply sighed. She rested her chin on her fist and stared at David as she shook her head. "I think I've done enough for myself today, Emma."

"You're not a happy woman, Gretchen?"

Gretchen looked at the innocent expression on David's face. "I'm feeling a bit foolish, but I'm okay. You won fair and square," she told the man who had known her better than she'd apparently known herself.

"And I intend to hold up my end of the bargain, sweet lady," he said. "We're going to enjoy ourselves at that wedding. We're going to make people talk. You can bet on that."

Gretchen couldn't hold back a small chuckle. "I think I've bet enough lately, David, so I'll take you at your word."

"You don't want me with you at the wedding?"

She looked across at the mischievous gleam in his eyes, at that bold I-dare-you-to-be-wild-and-crazy expression on his face, at the stunning magnificence of the man, and she shook her head.

"I'm beginning to think maybe I do want you at the wedding."

"We'll have fun, Gretchen."

And suddenly she was looking forward to the day she'd dreaded up until now. She had the feeling that David Hannon could turn any dull occasion into something special.

"Then I'll look forward to it," she agreed. "Partner."

He shook his head as Emma wandered off. "Not this time. This time we go as ourselves. A man and a woman."

And suddenly Gretchen felt as if everyone in the room faded away, as if she and David were alone. A man and a woman.

That feeling tagged after her all day as she and David returned to the office, made calls, and talked with each other and Rafe about Storm's likely whereabouts.

It was still with her when she wandered out onto the street at the end of the day, as she walked to her car, David at her side.

She reached down for the handle and suddenly his hand was over hers.

"Gretchen?"

She turned to look into his eyes, but he'd come up behind her and when she turned, she was almost up against him, her eyes just beneath his chin, her lips just a finger's breadth from his throat.

David groaned low.

"Come here," he said, slipping his arms around her. And it was as if she had been waiting for this for hours. She leaned nearer, went the extra distance to shape her lips to his own. She felt the world dissolve in heat and need as David moved in close and claimed her mouth again and again.

"I haven't kissed you in days," he whispered.

She nodded, kissing him again.

"We decided we shouldn't," she said, the words barely out of her mouth before she was crushed to his chest again.

"I know, but we weren't engaged then."

She smiled against his lips and placed her palms against the warmth of his chest. "David, we aren't engaged now," she said, finally pulling back slightly.

He smiled, snagging her for one more kiss. "Gretchen, you know that and I know that, but the world?" He brushed her jawline with his strong, gentle fingers. "What do you think the world thinks?"

Gretchen didn't know. Right this second she wasn't sure she cared. But she did know one thing. She and David were playing a game, and games always came to an end.

That was good, she reminded herself. That was the way she wanted things. Still…

"We're supposed to be pretending at the wedding, not here in town," she reminded him, disentangling herself from the warmth of his arms when what she wanted to do was to open his shirt, lean in and bury her face against the muscles of his bare chest. She wanted to breathe in the seductive male scent of him.

"I know that, love," he told her. "But I thought maybe we should practice."

A thought occurred to her. A niggling uncomfortable thought. "Not used to being without a woman for any length of time, David?"

His laugh was automatic. It rumbled through his body to her fingertips where her hand rested against his chest. "You think I have no self-control, Gretchen?"

She tilted up her chin. Green eyes met green eyes.

"I think you're a man who's used to getting his own way, David."

He sobered instantly. He took her hand in his own and kissed the pads of her fingertips. "I'm sorry I pushed myself on you on this case, Gretchen, but that has nothing to do with this."

She knew that. Deep inside she knew that. But she also knew that he was a man who was made to have his way with women, and she was a woman who was wary of getting too close to any one man. She would have to be very careful around David, she thought.

Gretchen wondered just how many women had thought that same thought over the years.

But she refused to guess at the number. This time with David could be simple if she made it that way. She could compartmentalize things. There was work with David and there was the David she was going to have a lark with at the wedding. That was all there was or ever would be for her and David Hannon.

And now that she'd set it out for herself so clearly, she could simply go home and forget about the man for the night.

The slight knock at her door that night startled Gretchen. She was just about to take Goliath for his evening walk. But when she pulled open the door, David was standing there.

He held out his hand.

She frowned. "David?"

He held out his hand farther. "The leash, Gretchen. The men are going for a walk. You stay here and rest."

Gretchen crossed her arms. "David, you won the bet."

Shaking his head, he gently pried the leash from her fingers. Goliath must have heard the noise of the door opening. He came running into the room, dancing and jumping and turning around in quick, chasing circles.

"Come on, boy, just you and me tonight," David said, lowering himself to one knee.

Gretchen knelt beside them. She placed her hand over David's and tried to ignore the warmth that cascaded through her in great gushing streams the way it always did.

"David, why are you doing this? I conceded. You won."

But he placed two fingers over her lips to shush her, a barely there touch that still left her longing for more.

"Not really a fair bet," he said quietly. "Anyone could have won it. Any man could see that a woman like you couldn't just leave Lily Mae sitting there babbling on."

Gretchen smiled against his fingertips.

"Are you telling me that you're not going through with things?" She wondered at the sudden plummeting of her good mood.

He gave her a lopsided, maddeningly sexy grin. "I said it was too easy, sweetheart. I didn't say I'd gone suddenly crazy and stupid. When a man wins first rights to spend an evening touching a woman like you and whirling around a dance floor with you next to his heart, he'd have to have misplaced his brain to give that up. Oh, no, no way am I giving up my winnings. I'm just making things a bit more fair."

Darn. She wished he wouldn't do that. He was hard enough to resist as it was.

"That doesn't seem half fair to you," she suggested. "No matter what you say, the bet was made, witnessed and won. And Goliath's *my* pet."

Of course, the darn animal was licking David's

fingers like crazy right now. The man was letting him, only stopping now and then to scratch Goliath's side.

"Well, maybe Goliath and I just need to spend some time together then. It's a guy thing," he told her. "This mutt definitely needs some male companionship. We won't be long, love," he told her. "You just get some rest."

And with that, he clipped the leash on and rose, swinging out the door and up the street.

They were gone for maybe twenty minutes, but Gretchen didn't rest. She paced. She cursed David for taking over her every thought. She blessed him for being so giving. She was just swishing past the window on her two hundredth pass when she saw him striding up her walk.

Gretchen pulled the door open wide. David didn't step inside. Instead he silently handed her the leash, said goodbye to Goliath, and gave her a slow smile.

That was all it took. One look. One smile. She opened her mouth, on the verge of inviting him in, of giving him coffee and anything else he should care to want, when he curled his palm around her jaw and gently brushed her lips with his thumb.

"See you in the morning, Gretchen," he said softly, thickly. "I'll be dreaming about you in my bed tonight."

And with those maddening words, the darn man left her standing there. Wanting. Hot and empty-handed and as far away from sleep as a woman could get. She'd just bet that he knew it, too.

Why, oh, why, had David Hannon come back home and walked into her police department and into the middle of her case?

Gretchen didn't know, but she knew one thing. She

was for darn sure going to be glad when he went back into his world and left hers behind, glad when she could get back to the life where she was a lot more in control than she ever was here. Until then, she was just going to—well, heck, she was just going to enjoy her time with the man, wasn't she? And there was no use lying to herself about it. He was, after all, exactly what she was always saying she wanted. A man who knew when to have fun and when to disappear into the mists of history.

Four days later David was on the phone in the station trying to keep his hand in on one of his own federal cases when he heard the commotion at the front door. "I want to see Detective Neal." A man's low voice echoed throughout the office. It wasn't a happy voice. One might even say it sounded a bit threatening.

Immediately David looked to his right to where Gretchen was scratching away on paper. Her hand still, she looked up and rose to her feet, just as if some candy-voiced grandmother was sweetly requesting her presence.

"Royston, got an unexpected emergency here. I'll call you back ASAP," David said quietly into the phone, not waiting for his contact's reply as he placed the receiver back in its cradle.

Carefully and deliberately, he rose from his desk and proceeded into the other room.

"You Detective Neal?" a tall, brown-eyed man was demanding. His long, black hair was graying slightly at the temples, slicked back in magazine-model style, his Native American ancestry evident in the chiseled cheekbones. His navy pin-striped suit was expensive and it fit his broad-shouldered, narrow-hipped frame well. He was obviously at home in a three-piece, and David didn't have to ask who the man was. He was the very image of what Raven Hunter would have looked like had he lived, and the word "attorney" was practically stamped on the guy's forehead.

David leaned back against the nearest bank of file cabinets, his arms crossed at his chest. Storm Hunter might have come in full courtroom battle dress, but he hadn't matched wits with Gretchen Neal before. A small smile lifted David's lips as Gretchen stepped forward.

"I'm Detective Neal," she said, holding out her hand.

The man simply thinned his lips and took a step forward into her space. He didn't take the hand she offered.

"I want to know what's going on regarding the murder of my brother, Raven Hunter," he said.

"The case is being investigated," Gretchen said calmly. "Why don't you step into my office?"

"Why don't you explain why you haven't already reached some conclusion considering the circumstances?"

She raised one brow. "The circumstances being?"

"It's been quite a while since the remains were found. It's no secret to anyone in this town that Jeremiah Kincaid hated the fact that my brother, a member of a race he despised, was fooling around with Kincaid's sister. Nor is it a secret that he had words with Raven just before my brother disappeared. And yet I understand you're no closer to the truth than you were when you started."

"It's an old case with all the complications of an old

case," Gretchen said, stepping forward herself. "Convictions can't be made on hearsay, Mr. Hunter, as you well know. We need hard evidence. More evidence than we have. I understand your concern, but—"

"You understand nothing. It's clear to me that you're *doing* nothing. In fact, it's come to my attention today that you may be in collusion with the nephew of the man suspected of killing my brother."

David's arms came uncrossed. He straightened. Only Gretchen's brief shake of her head in his direction kept him from stepping in to open his mouth.

"The case is proceeding," Gretchen said, swigging in a deep breath of air and pulling herself up to her full five feet, nine inches. "And it's being given my full attention. We're looking for new evidence all the time. The department is doing everything it can to discover the truth here, Mr. Hunter, as expediently as possible."

The man was shaking his head, slowly, deliberately. "Not good enough, Neal. If Raven had been white, you would have moved faster. You would have been working on this thing 'round the clock. Your prejudices are showing. Alarmingly so, Ms. Neal."

"I'm sorry you feel that way, but you're wrong, Mr. Hunter."

"You're a disgrace."

The man's words hung in the silent air that had suddenly dropped over the station. All eyes were turned toward Gretchen and Storm.

"I want answers, Neal," the man continued. "And I want them now. If I don't get them in a timely fashion, then I want your badge. And I'll have it."

Gretchen raised her chin, her breath coming more quickly though her expression was one of calm determination. She opened her mouth, but David had had enough.

"You've taken this a notch too far, Hunter. You don't know what you're talking about here," he said, his voice a low, quiet command in the silent room. David ignored the halting look in Gretchen's eyes. He moved into the arena.

"Ah, the good detective's boyfriend speaks." Storm sneered the words. Ice hung in the air around him. "You like Kincaids, Detective Neal?" he continued. "That's what Agent Hannon is, after all, isn't he? I've only been in town a few minutes, just stopped by the café for coffee, but already I've heard that the two of you are pretty tight and hot. Well, no surprise. The Kincaids have always had favored status in this town. Not like the Hunters. Oh, no. It was your uncle that threatened my brother, Hannon, and now I'm going to threaten your woman. I don't particularly care what she does in your bed at night, but she does her job or she loses it."

A flashfire of darkness spiraled through David. He'd been good too long. He'd held back to keep from causing Gretchen any distress. He knew from experience that she could kick the life out of this man—and that she wouldn't. Of course she wouldn't. Because she had no right to touch him in that way just to defend her honor. And because that was just the kind of woman she was. Right now she was probably imagining all the horrible things Storm had probably gone through that had turned him into this bitter, insulting human. She was probably right. David was damn sure she was right.

"My uncle was a sorry excuse for a human being, Hunter, and yes, there've been times when I hated to admit that I was related to him, but you're out of line insulting Detective Neal. She's a fine detective and a wonderful human being. Now why don't you get smart and take back all the insulting things you just said about her, because her hands may be tied by her office, but mine are free. And I happen to be off duty."

"That's good, Kincaid. Very good," Storm said, yanking on his tie. "Because I'm in just the right mood to match my fists against that pretty face of yours."

And in the next split second, he doubled up his fist and aimed.

David dodged, the air buckling next to his jaw as the man's blow barely missed. He tried to quell the roar of anger and to remember all the things that Gretchen would have said about Storm Hunter; that he had a right to be angry, that they had a duty to let him say his piece. But David had lived on the edge for a long time. He'd been in more fights for his life than he cared to count, and his fingers curled easily and eagerly into fists as Storm recovered and prepared to strike again.

"Hunter, stop right there or you'll find yourself in lockup overnight." Rafe Rawlings's voice carried through the panting stillness.

The world froze for five whole seconds. The fire still burned, but the flames died down slightly. Counting to ten, to twenty, to thirty, David finally, slowly, unfurled his fists.

Storm pulled back. He gave David a disgusted look. "Later," he mouthed.

David raised one brow. "Your call, buddy," he said.

"Hannon, you're here on my recognizance. I'd appreciate it if you'd remember that," Rafe said quietly.

David remembered, and he remembered the debt of gratitude he owed Rafe and also Phil for looking the

other way to let him be here. Nor did he forget that
Gretchen would be humiliated if he got into a fight
over her in her very own station.

Slowly, he relaxed his muscles and backed away a
step or two.

"Storm, you're out of line," Rafe said, stepping in to
take over. "You have every right to ask questions, but
this is going too far."

"You're going to deny that this investigation is at a
virtual standstill?"

"Absolutely not. As I'm sure Gretchen told you,
the investigation is continuing, but we don't have
much to go on."

"You've got my brother's remains and the knowledge that there was a lot going on between him and
Blanche Kincaid just before Raven disappeared."

"We have that," Gretchen said, giving Rafe an apologetic look. She was grateful to him for his presence that
had somewhat diffused the situation. But Raven Hunter
was her case, and it was up to her to deal with Storm.
"And we've interviewed what witnesses we can find to
tell us about what was going on at that time. Yes, Raven
and Jeremiah were at odds. Yes, Raven disappeared. Yes,
Blanche gave birth to your niece, Summer. And yes,
there's a possibility that the murder weapon could have
come from Jeremiah's collection, but we don't have con-
clusive evidence. As an attorney, I'm sure you understand the importance of gathering accurate information."

"We were hoping you could provide more details,
Storm," Rafe said lazily. "We've been waiting for you
to get your tail back here so we could ask you a few
things. I understand Jackson contacted you three
weeks ago."

A dark rash of color climbed Storm's face. "I've had cases pending in New Mexico. It was difficult to get away."

Gretchen raised one brow. She glanced toward the phone. "You could have called," she said, her tone somewhat lazy and accusatory. "But then, maybe you wanted to be here in person. Maybe you had a lot you needed to get off your chest. A man's brother goes missing and everyone thinks he ran away, it would raise a lot of anger to find out that man had actually been murdered. Probably dredge up a lot of pain he'd already gone through once before and thought he'd put behind him, as well."

"Don't be patronizing, Detective Neal."

She shook her head. "Believe me, I'm not being patronizing, Mr. Hunter. I'm just stating the truth. Maybe you had your own reasons for waiting to speak to us in person."

Storm took a deep breath and eyed her somewhat suspiciously. Then the smallest light of respect edged into his eyes. "All right. We'll talk. I'll tell you what little I know," he agreed.

David stepped forward, prepared to demand that the man apologize to Gretchen, but she stopped him dead with that "Don't even think of it," look she managed so well.

Shrugging, David grinned. He trailed the two of them into Gretchen's office.

"He have to be here?" Storm demanded.

"He's on the case," Gretchen answered quietly. "What I know and Rafe knows, he knows."

Storm held out his hands in sullen surrender. He shot David one last accusatory look. Then he began to talk.

* * *

All right, so reality was finally beginning to sink in, Gretchen realized, curling her trembling hand more tightly around her coffee cup, then quickly glancing David's way to make sure he hadn't noticed.

His eyes flashed dark green sparks. "Let's get out of here," he growled, reaching for her as he climbed to his feet. "The day's gone on too long, and in the end, Storm Hunter really didn't tell us anything we didn't already know."

"Except that he's one very angry man," Gretchen said flippantly, stepping out into the aisle herself. She purposely held her hand at her side.

He stared pointedly at where she'd folded her closed fingers against the dark cloth of her pants.

"Lots of officers would have quaked under that kind of abuse," he said quietly.

She gave a small laugh. "You don't have to pat me on the head, David. I'm sure you've had more than your share of people spitting into your face. That comes with the badge."

"Maybe so, but no one ever said it was one of the more pleasant aspects of the law enforcement business." He waited for her to gather her gear, then strolled out of the office beside her.

It pleased her that he didn't try to baby her as they left the station. He didn't treat her as if she were some fragile female, even though he'd obviously wanted to give Storm a body slam earlier today. He'd wanted to, but he hadn't.

"Thanks," she said quietly as they climbed into the car.

He raised both brows, but didn't ask what she meant.

"You know what I'm talking about, Hannon. You grew up in a house filled with ladies who probably loved having you play the perfect gentleman. Your mother is a wonderful woman, a strong woman, and an absolute sweetheart, but don't tell me that those traditional male and female roles didn't exist in your household. You were born opening doors for women and kissing their hands. I'm sure it took a lot to keep you from defending my honor today."

He gave a harsh laugh. "Don't thank me. Thank Rafe. I was ready to deck Hunter and you know it."

She smiled. "Yes, but you were mulling the situation over. I could see it in the tense cords in your neck. You could have easily flattened him by the time Rafe entered the room, but something held you back. I suspect it was concern for my position."

He turned to the side, but she didn't miss the slow smile that eased onto his lips. "You think you know me, do you?"

She shook her head. "No, but I'm beginning to. Your natural inclination is to come to a lady's rescue. You've done it any number of times with me, but today, when it counted, when my ability to handle my job was in question, you held back. I'd like to think it was because you respected me."

"Don't ever think I don't." The smile had disappeared when he swung back around. "But don't make the mistake of thinking that it was easy, either. Nothing's easy with you, Gretchen. I wanted that guy's blood."

"I could see that, and I can see that it cost you to back away. You've still got some of that residual anger bottled up inside you. Well, if it makes you feel any better, you did come to my rescue today. Just knowing that I wasn't alone made it easier than it's ever been before."

He closed his eyes. "Don't. Don't tell me about the times you've had maniacs waving fists or guns or knives in your face. Working where you have, doing what you do, I'm sure it's happened, but today…just don't, because yes, I'm still angry and frustrated and— Damn it, Gretchen."

David reached across the seat, looped his hands around her waist and lifted her up and over onto his lap. His fingers speared through her hair, his seeking mouth found hers. He wrapped her around him and held her tightly as he plunged them both into sudden and reckless sensation.

The heat of his touch seared her, and Gretchen struggled to get closer. She squirmed against his hard chest, bringing her hands up to wrap around his neck and bind him to her. Seated in the tight confines of the car, she nevertheless felt as if she were falling off a high tower.

Exhilaration flooded her soul as David pulled back for air and then swooped her hard against him again and kissed her over and over.

"You make me crazy," he whispered.

"You make me shiver," she whispered back, and some small part of her realized it was true. She was shaking, literally shaking, in David's arms. His kisses had done what all of Storm's gibes hadn't done. Made her quake. With desire. With need. And with the fear of the unknown.

Someday soon, she was going to be on her own again, as she'd known she would be all her life. As she wanted to be.

She hoped, really hoped, that David's touch hadn't spoiled her for life. And once again, as she finally pulled away from the embrace, she wondered just what kind of trouble she was getting into with David. For delicious as it was, she was sure it was trouble. And it was obviously trouble she wasn't resisting very well. Tomorrow she and David were going to pretend to get engaged. She must have been completely out of control when she agreed to that bet, but she *had* agreed and all she could do now was simply plunge in.

Eight

He'd done some outrageous things in his time, but this probably qualified as one of the more outrageous situations he'd engineered, David admitted to himself the next day. He threw his clothes into a bag, preparing for the wedding in Helena he and Gretchen would be driving to after work. Not that he'd ever followed the crowd in the usual way of things. His parents had been too much the free spirits and he'd been forced into that loner pathway much too early to have ever become a slave to convention, but...there was something about Gretchen that just made him act wilder than usual.

He was obviously not in control of his reactions where the woman was concerned. He couldn't seem to keep his hands off her—or his thoughts from her. She made him want things, things he didn't even want to think about, given the circumstances. He had to be careful with her. She was more vulnerable than she wanted to let on and she was prickly about getting involved. If he pushed, he could do her damage and there were already more than enough people taking advantage of her, even some who might want to hurt her.

Storm Hunter's angry face slipped into his mind, but it wasn't really Storm he was angry with. It was himself he wanted to beat up on. He was, after all, the one who had made her a target of Storm Hunter's ire both because of his Kincaid connections and because of his having kissed her in public.

"And yet you did it again not four hours after Hunter left the office," he chastised himself. "And here you are luring the woman into this fake fiancé charade. Don't you feel guilty, bud?"

He let up on himself, relaxed into the truth. And the truth was…? He grinned. No, he didn't have an iota of guilt about going off with Gretchen to pretend he was more involved with her than he was. Because this weekend he was going to have Gretchen in his arms for hours. At least on the dance floor. Later, maybe, he'd feel guilty about his tendency to publicly plaster his body to hers.

"You ready for this weekend?" he asked her as he breezed into the station and plopped down into the chair beside her desk.

Her smile was slightly taut. "I think it's finally sinking in just what we're planning to do. You should probably be aware, David, that I'm not particularly gifted in the field of acting."

"You don't have to be. Just follow my lead. I'm willing to shoulder the responsibility. All you have to do is give me the occasional adoring look. Think you can manage that?"

He grinned and winked at her, and she rolled her eyes, grinning back. "I'm not sure. How does this look?" And she framed her face with both hands, opened her sea-green eyes wide and parted her lips slightly, leaning forward in his direction.

His own grin faded. He swallowed hard. "That'll do, Gretchen," he whispered, rising to lean over her desk. "That'll do very nicely."

He bent over slightly, looked straight into those beautiful eyes, lifted his hand with every intention of cupping the soft skin of her cheek.

"Oh, excuse me. I just keep managing to come in at the oddest moments, don't I?" Celeste's nervous voice filled the small space of the office.

David quickly rose to his full height. He stepped in front of Gretchen to give her a chance to put her detective persona back in place.

"Don't worry, Aunt Celeste. Gretchen and I were just doing a little role-playing. It comes in handy now and then."

His aunt blinked, then smiled brightly. "Well, of course it does. I suppose law enforcement people have to go undercover now and then, don't they? I knew that. Everyone knows that, don't they?"

David wanted to laugh at the way his aunt was trying to be so accommodating. He wondered if she really believed his story about role-playing.

He couldn't tell, but he knew he had to be more careful around Gretchen. At least at work. He didn't really care what people said or thought, but he had the distinct feeling that she did. He'd do his best not to bring her any grief.

"You're still leaving for the weekend, David?"

Celeste asked with a smile, moving forward into the room. "Gretchen's wedding, isn't it?" She waited, her eyes wide and expectant.

"A friend of hers, yes."

"Well, you two just have a lot of fun there," she ordered. "Not that I think you won't. I'm sure it'll be nice to get away from all this trouble for a bit."

He grinned at his aunt. "I remember you once telling me that I seemed to court trouble, one long ago day when I got into some sort of mischief."

Celeste smiled. "Well, yes, but this is different. I know it's the work you've both chosen, but hunting for murderers just can't be as much fun as going to a celebration. You just don't even think about anything except for that wedding while you're there. I want you to have fun, to just be free," she commanded.

She looked at him pointedly.

He grinned. "Yes, ma'am," he answered in the way he had once been wont to do as a child.

She sighed. "I guess you're right. You're too old to have me ordering you around. And anyway, that's not really what I came to talk to you about. I'm…well, I'm just on my way out to the reservation, dear. You know that I sometimes volunteer at the youth center there, and this summer they're having a special program on careers. I'm helping out a bit with some of the research, locating materials and so forth. I was thinking…well, I was thinking of approaching Mr. Hunter. He's an attorney doing some special work in civil liberties, you know. He's been gone all those years. I hear he was in here yesterday. I was wondering what your impression of him might be. Maybe you could tell me something about him."

David frowned, shaking his head in confusion. "I think that while Storm Hunter might be a font of information on the topic you're researching, you would be the wrong person to ask him for help. He has an aversion to anyone associated with the Kincaids."

Celeste took in a long breath. She folded her hands tightly around each other. "He said things to you, then? What did he say?"

David shook his head. "You know that I can't discuss a case with you, Aunt Celeste. But just be warned, this is the wrong time to go asking Storm Hunter for a favor. If you need his help for the school, get Jackson to approach him."

"He didn't threaten you, did he?" She had asked the question of David, but she was looking at Gretchen as if she hoped she'd get more information there. Gretchen, true to her professionalism, didn't blink an eye.

"Jackson's very approachable, Celeste," she said gently. "You know that. He and his wife, Maggie, are quite involved with the school, I believe?"

Slowly, Celeste nodded and then let out a sigh. "All right. Of course, you're right. I just thought that if Mr. Hunter is only going to be in town a short while, that maybe we shouldn't waste the opportunity, but of course, Jackson would be the logical person for me to talk to about this. I'll just talk to him. You two enjoy the wedding. And don't let anything stop you from going."

And she squared her shoulders and walked out the door.

Gretchen watched her go, wondering at that strange last comment. Celeste had certainly seemed happy to see them going off for the weekend together, but of course that was probably just her imagination going wild, she told herself. Celeste couldn't know about the pretend engagement and she wasn't the type to push two people together who didn't want to be pushed. She was just a kind woman, a caring aunt. And Gretchen had to admire the woman's strength and determination. "Your aunt's been involved with events on the reservation for a long while, hasn't she?"

David shrugged. "She's always said that she was fortunate to have such access to two cultures. She and my mother raised my cousin, Summer, Blanche's and Raven's daughter, and Summer spent every summer break on the reservation. Those of us who know and love Summer and have the good fortune to be related to her have been blessed to have been able to walk between both worlds more than most of the people in the town. Still, it's a bit worrisome to have Aunt Celeste asking about Storm. I have the feeling that she's worrying about my safety. Even if Jeremiah isn't proven to be Raven's murderer, there's definitely a lot to be accounted for there. No matter how angry I was with Storm yesterday, the man does have every reason to be bitter."

"David, you can't be responsible for your uncle's character."

He held out his hands in a gesture of defeat. "I know that. If I were responsible for all the misery Jeremiah caused, I would have had to go into therapy the moment I came out of the womb. Jeremiah left illegitimate children, unhappy women and so much dirt in his wake, that I'd never be able to atone for all his sins. The Kincaids may be proud, but we've always known that there are plenty of people who have reason to resent our name."

"But not you."

"I hope not, Gretchen. I do my best to walk a straight line and not cause the same kinds of trouble Jeremiah caused."

Ah, so he was worrying if all his teasing and flirting was going a bit too far. She wasn't sure. She knew that he was just kidding with her, that he desired her, but that there were limits. Heaven knew she had loads of limits of her own. She didn't want him worrying about her.

"You're interested only in protecting your good name? So that's why you rescue women in distress?" she teased.

He gave her a lazy grin, settled one hip on the edge of her desk and leaned over her.

"I do that just because it's so much fun. You going to stir up some trouble on the streets today so I can watch you work? I get excited just thinking about you kicking some guy up alongside his head. You could have made some football team very happy."

She rose up and met him eye-to-eye. "Maybe I did. My brothers regularly called me in as a kicker when they played with their friends. And if watching me work makes your heart sit up and smile, then prepare yourself, Hannon, because I have a treat coming up for you in a few days. Rafe just gave me this assignment this morning."

He looked down at the paper she was holding out to him.

Long seconds ticked by as he read what was written there. And then read it again.

"Excuse me," he finally said. "Maybe I misunderstood this directive. We're giving a talk at the school? You and me?"

"I know," she said with a teasing whisper. "Kind of makes you shiver with anticipation, doesn't it?"

He laughed out loud. "I'm not so sure about that."

She chuckled right back. "Well, I'm looking forward to watching you charm the hearts of a squirming roomful of ten-year-olds, David. I've watched you turn women into melted butter, coax cats out of trees, and make grown men rethink their position on crime. I can't wait to see you interact with the peanut-butter-and-jelly crowd."

David raised both brows. "Somehow I have the feeling you've done this before."

She nodded slowly, her eyes wide.

"So you know what I'm in for?"

Gretchen shrugged. "Every year is different. Different crop of kids, different situations."

He studied her carefully. "You know what I told you about just following my lead this weekend?"

She nodded. "Yes. Why?"

"Just remember that when we get to that school. You lead. I'll follow."

A slow smile formed on her face. "That's the sexiest thing you've ever said to me, Hannon."

He gave her another wink. "Just wait until we get to this wedding. I intend to say a few more sexy things to you. Get ready."

Celeste sat in her car on the shoulder of the highway after her meeting with David and Gretchen. In a minute she would get going. She couldn't sit here much longer. If she did, someone would come along and ask her if she needed help.

She did need help, but she'd learned long ago that the only kind of help that would ever save her was the divine kind. In time, someday, maybe someday soon, there would be a spiritual reckoning for her, a day when she could finally, really, find out what had happened that long-ago night and what was in store for her for eternity. In the meantime, all she could do was try her best to go on and to look out for those she loved.

"David is trying to open up the past, figure out what happened? And what *did* happen? What is he going to dig up? And how is that going to affect all of us?" she whispered out loud.

"I just wish I could do something. I wish I could somehow protect all of them."

She had the horrid, sinking feeling that her children, Cleo and Jasmine, were going to be hurt by whatever news was found. And David, too. If he found anything that would damage his family, what would it do to him? Jeremiah was being blamed and Jeremiah had been a miserable human being, but had he really been a murderer?

She was afraid to find out the answer to that question and afraid not to.

Her niece, Summer, had lived a life without a father because of what had happened so long ago. Storm Hunter had lost a brother, and someone should have to pay for that. The killer should be discovered and revealed to the world.

But the thought of that nearly made Celeste double over with pain.

Someone had a lot to answer for. And somewhere in the darkness of those dreams that haunted her, the answers to who that someone was waited.

But those answers were closed to her. She had to

keep searching. In the meantime, all she could do was try to shield those closest to her from the truth and to pray that Storm Hunter found some happiness in his life someday.

"Gretchen!" The curvy brunette standing in the hotel lobby came running across the floor not five minutes after David and Gretchen had arrived. She held out her arms and Gretchen gave her a big hug.

"Karen. It's so good to see you. We've had so little time to talk lately, between your job and mine." Gretchen turned to David, inviting him into the circle with her friend. "David, this is Karen Warren, my very good friend from Miami and another one of Pamela's bridesmaids. Karen, this is David Hannon, my—my fiancé."

Karen let out a scream that could probably be heard all the way back in Whitehorn. "Gretchen, you're engaged! Finally? Why didn't you tell anyone? You didn't tell anyone, did you? I'm not the last to know?"

Gretchen shook her head as David chuckled and took Karen's hand. "It's very nice to meet someone from Gretchen's other life. I suppose you're the journalist?"

The woman nodded with a huge smile. "She told you about me? Oh, Gretchen, that's sweet."

"Of course I told him about you, Karen. You're one of my very closest friends and David is, as I said, my…"

"Fiancé, love," David supplied when she faltered. "I'm afraid our engagement has taken Gretchen a bit by surprise," he said apologetically. "It's pretty new to both of us. In fact, you're probably the first to know."

"Oh, David, allow me to congratulate you for doing

what no man has ever done before," Karen said, rising on her toes to kiss his cheek. "You've managed to win our Gretchen's heart. I hope you appreciate the magnitude of what you've accomplished and the gift that she's given you."

"She's an absolute treasure," he said, pulling Gretchen's hand beneath his arm. "I thank the heavens every day for dropping me into her life and giving me this rare opportunity."

He smiled down at Gretchen and her breath caught in her throat. Horrid man. If only Karen knew that this rare opportunity referred to his chance to play this charade with her and not to the fact that they were engaged. She was grateful, of course. It was already obvious that this wedding was going to be more fun and much less tension-filled than those in recent memory, but she really shouldn't let David carry this too far.

Karen almost sighed and Gretchen felt a small moment's irritation at the dreamlike way her friend was looking at David.

"How did he propose? Come on now, you can tell me," Karen prompted.

David opened his mouth to speak, but Gretchen placed her hand gently on his cheek. "Let me relive it, darling," she coaxed.

He raised one brow. "You don't know how much I'd love that," he whispered back.

Gretchen looked around to see if anyone else was listening even though she knew that the story would be retold many times. Karen was a hopeless romantic and an equally hopeless gossip.

She looked up at him and hoped she wasn't blushing. Then she lifted one shoulder and plunged ahead.

"David knows how much I love white roses. He filled my room with them when I was away and then, when we went back to my apartment later, he went down on one knee and presented me with another rose. Red. He kissed it and gave it to me. My ring was enclosed in the petals."

Looking up at David, Gretchen saw that he was grinning broadly. Had she taken this too far? She knew she had agreed to let him lead. Indeed, she'd even wanted him to a few days ago, but there was just something about this strange relationship they had, this constant tussle to figure out who was leading and who was following, that made it impossible for her to simply remain a spectator at her own pretend engagement. It was generous of David to offer to help her, but darn it, she was no coward. She had to jump right into the thick of the action, just as she always had. She couldn't let someone else call all the shots.

"Isn't that the way you remember it, David?" she asked tentatively.

"Mmm. I remember it just like that," he said in that low, sexy voice. "Except in my memory you were wearing nothing but rose petals and I kissed you deeply just before I gave you the ring."

She gave him a laser-eyed look that said, "Freeze, buddy."

"David, you're wicked. You'll embarrass Karen," she said in reality.

But Karen was beyond being embarrassed. The lady closed her eyes and let out such a long sigh that for a moment Gretchen was afraid she was going to faint. Then her friend looked down.

"That's so-oo-o romantic, Gretchen. But where's your ring?"

Oh, darn it. She'd gotten so caught up in trying to one-up David that she had embellished this tale just a bit too much. Gretchen looked at her hand as if it belonged to another woman. "I—"

"I have it right here, love," David said, reaching into his pocket. "Gretchen doesn't wear her ring at work. It might get caught on something and be a danger to her."

"Of course," Karen agreed immediately, "but you're not on duty now, Gretchen."

Gretchen smiled wanly at her friend. Oh, no, now what was David going to say? He didn't really have a ring in his pocket.

But the darn man came up from the depths of his pocket with a slender, diamond-and-emerald-studded band. Taking her cold hand in his own, he slipped the ring possessively on her finger, then kissed her palm.

Hot flames shot up through her body.

"So nice to meet you, Karen," he said softly, "We'll see you later, after Gretchen and I have time to settle in and get comfortable. Shall we?"

Karen smiled knowingly. "By all means, you two just go on up to your rooms. I'll see you at the rehearsal dinner and at the wedding. And don't worry, Gretchen. You know me. I won't tell a soul about your engagement."

Gretchen gave her friend another hug and watched her walk away. "I feel rather guilty. Karen's always loved romance. She's been engaged and had her heart broken several times. How's she going to feel when she finds out I'm not really engaged? She's my friend."

"Yes, she's your friend and she wants you to be happy," David said gently. "And it's obvious that to Karen, being happy means being in love. So she'll understand that you just wanted to experience that glow for a short time, even if you tell her that it wasn't real. She may not believe that it's pretend, even if you tell her the truth. Some people just want to see what makes them happy. Your friends want to see you happy. So be happy. Let them enjoy this brief time. We *are* engaged, as far as I'm concerned. We're simply engaged for the duration of this trip."

She chuckled. "That sounds devious, but I like it. It works for me. If I could have gotten engaged for a mere weekend before, I might have already done so."

He widened his eyes and tilted his head. "Gretchen, are you telling me you would agree to marry another man when I've just now slipped my ring on your finger?" He took her hand into his own and slowly kissed the pads of each finger.

Gretchen dragged in a long breath, curving her fingers closed lightly. She hazarded a hesitant smile his way. "No, David," she said softly. "I can guarantee that this weekend is all there'll ever be. You're the only man whose ring I'll ever wear."

He nodded, a slight frown forming between his eyes. "Come on, love."

"Where are we going?"

"To your room."

He tugged on her hand, but she pulled back. If she allowed David to come to her room, a regular hotel room with not much more than a bed in it, she wasn't sure if she'd be able to keep from letting the inevitable happen this time.

"Why my room?" She still hadn't moved.

He gave a harder tug and she came up against his chest. He kissed her gently. "Because Karen has already told a large group of people that we're engaged and some of them are looking somewhat skeptical," he whispered against her mouth, tensing a shoulder in the direction her friend had wandered off to. "No, don't look unless you want them to realize we're putting on a show."

She kissed him back. "So we're running away to hide in my room, David?"

He laughed against her lips, his breath a warm caress. "We're going to let them wonder what we're doing up there."

"I don't think they'll be doing much wondering. All of them will be sure we're making love."

He raised one brow. "Do you really think so? How shocking."

"Yes, isn't it?" she said, placing her hands on his chest and smiling up at him.

"You wouldn't be in the mood to add a little shocking fuel to the fire, would you? To seal our fate, to make everyone truly believe that the elusive Gretchen Neal has finally been captured?"

She rose up on her toes and kissed his lips. "You want to go to our room, David?" she said loudly enough for those nearby to hear. "That's a wonderful idea, my love."

Allowing him to lead her toward the elevators, she pretended she didn't know that the mother of the bride was on the way over to talk to her. The idea had been to enjoy themselves, to let everyone think that this time it would be a mistake for anyone to try to fix her up with a man.

But moving ever closer to her room with David, Gretchen wondered if she wasn't making an even bigger mistake.

Nine

He had to be certifiably insane to think he could get away with this, David thought, entering Gretchen's room. The masquerade had been his idea, simply a way to give Gretchen a break from all the matchmaking her well-meaning family and friends would have provided had she come alone.

But that wasn't exactly the complete truth, he admitted for the first time. The truth was that he wasn't sure he could have dealt with sitting back in Whitehorn while good-looking men were marched out for Gretchen's perusal. He'd had her in his sights for weeks now. He wanted her in his bed before he went back to Atlanta, and now that he was alone with her in a room with a king-size bed there was no denying the fact that he wanted very badly to touch her in the most intimate of ways. Immediately.

"They didn't have any doubles by the time I

booked," she explained as if he'd asked a question. "I—I didn't request this."

He almost groaned out loud. Just thinking of Gretchen naked and alone in a bed big enough for two to roll around in comfortably was making him a little crazy. He took a step in her direction.

She stood her ground, but she crossed her arms over her chest. "I can't believe you bought a ring."

"It was nothing."

"A diamond engagement ring isn't nothing."

"A necessity then," he conceded. "Adds a touch of reality."

She raised one delicately arched brow. "Just how far are you willing to go to add a touch of reality?"

"You don't like pretending, do you, Gretchen?"

A long sigh slipped through her lips. "It's not that. This could be fun, but—"

"But?"

She leaned back on the long bureau that ran the length of the room. "You and I— There's clearly… something between us."

"Salsa. Steam baths. Molten lava," he agreed.

"Things do tend to heat up when I'm with you," she conceded, "and that's a problem. It complicates the issues, the case."

"You think that maybe Storm is right, that I'm trying to influence you?"

She shook her head. "Actually, I don't, but I'm not so positive that I won't be influenced. I'm very loyal to my friends. That's why I never mix business and pleasure."

He fixed his dark green feral gaze on her. "And yet we're here. Together."

"I know. This probably wasn't very wise."

"You want out? We could tell everyone the truth."

A long, slow smile lifted her lips. "Over my dead body, Hannon. I intend to have fun this weekend. This is the first time in a long time I'll be able to attend a wedding without the vultures circling. If you think I'm going to give that up so easily, you're wrong."

He waited. She clearly had more to say.

"But this unexpected good fortune of mine *was* just the result of a simple bet," she said carefully. "We pretend. We let everyone else believe we're engaged, but we don't take it any further than we need to."

"You can't pretend away the mutual attraction, Gretchen." The darn man's smile was deep and lazy.

"I'm not trying to."

"What are you trying to do?"

A slight hesitation. "I'm trying to wait it out."

"You're uncomfortable."

"Of course I'm uncomfortable. It's bad enough that you and I are collaborating on a murder investigation where your uncle is the prime suspect. Complicating that with sex only makes things that much worse."

"Or better."

She sucked in a deep breath. Her hands shook slightly. And it was that little detail that made him swear at himself beneath his breath.

"Sit down, Gretchen. We'll make it right." He motioned toward the bed.

"I don't think—"

"I won't touch you," he promised. "Unless you ask me to. For now we'll just talk until enough time has passed and it won't look strange if I go back to my room alone."

"Talk about what?"

"Not about how I'd like to slowly slip open every tiny button on that dress you're wearing," he said. "Or how I'm dying to taste the softest part of your inner thigh."

She clenched her hands at her waist as her color rose.

"What, then?"

He sat on the bed, at the farthest end, and waited for her to join him there. "For now we'll just stick to the basics. Tell me about all the places you traveled to as a child. Tell me what you were like and who your friends were and what you did. Tell me what you were like as a teenager."

"I was busy."

"I'm sure you were. Your parents must have gone mad trying to keep the guys away. Mace. Sledgehammers. I'll bet your father had a whole arsenal of weapons to make sure your boyfriends brought you home on time and untouched."

She wrinkled her nose. "I really didn't get out all that much."

Something about the way she said that caught David square in the chest. "Maybe you should clarify that, love. You *did* get out? Group dates? Movies? Letting the boy next to you steal your popcorn?"

"David," she said sternly. "Don't sound so worried. It wasn't that my parents kept me locked up or anything like that. Or that I was some sort of prude. There just wasn't all that much time."

"Ah," he said gently. "All the brothers and sisters. That nurturing side of you."

She shrugged. "My parents weren't trying to deprive me. They were just overwhelmed themselves a lot of the time, I think. It takes a lot of time and work and money to raise a big family. My help was appreciated. It was welcome, and really, things got easier as the kids got older. I dated plenty once I went away to college."

"I'm sure you made up for lost time," he agreed, giving her the simple answer he figured she wanted to hear. He wasn't really sure he should have gone down this road in the first place. Now that he'd started, he figured it wouldn't be all that smart for him to hear the details of Gretchen's sexual awakening.

She must have known what he was thinking. She leveled a long, sexy, assessing glance at him, then raised one delicate brow. "Oh, yes, I made up for lost time. In fact, I was practically an animal, David. My studies suffered. Men were like sinful chocolate for me. I couldn't get enough."

"That bad?" he asked with a lazy smile.

She laughed and threw a pillow at him. "No, not that bad at all. I was very studious, but I dated some. And no, I'm not going into details."

"Probably just as well. I'd hate to have to go out looking for some guy you dated ten years ago with the aim of moving his nose from one side of his face to the other. Might be embarrassing. Maybe you'd better skip the dating years and just tell me about your childhood."

She edged nearer to the bed and settled herself against the headboard, looking down at him with an indulgent smile. "All right, then. I'll tell you. Will it surprise you to learn that I was a bossy child?"

He chuckled. "It would absolutely astound me."

She chuckled back. "And were you always as persuasive as you are now? I can't believe you talked me into telling you anything at all about my awkward social debut."

"Persuasive? Mmm, I suppose so. I talked my third grade teacher into letting me lead the investigation of who was stealing the lunches from everyone's lockers."

"Impressive. Did you solve the crime?"

"The case is still on the elementary school's books." His smile didn't tell her anything, at least not too much.

"You solved it, but you didn't turn the culprit in," she guessed.

He shrugged. "Extenuating circumstances. He needed the food. I merely made a deal. I brought an extra lunch for him for a while and he swept floors at the Big Sky until he made enough money to slip some pennies back into the lockers of the kids he'd stolen from. Not exactly the usual way of doing things, but a lot more rewarding and fun."

She nodded her agreement. "Too bad more crimes can't be atoned for that way."

He frowned. "Yes, it is too bad. No way we can bring back Raven Hunter. Storm's lost his brother. Summer's lost her father. And the killer may well be a dead man."

"But at least Storm and Summer will have some sort of closure."

His laugh was harsh. "When she was growing up, Summer wanted a father, not closure. But yes, I know you're right. Closure is the best we can hope for in this case. For Storm and Summer. For Celeste. For all of us. Not quite as satisfying as taking some drug-runners out of commission, but I guess it'll have to do."

"And we'll do it," she promised him. "Celeste and Summer and Storm will at least have knowledge, David."

"Mmm. They'll have that. And so will I. About you. Now tell me again, how bossy were you when you were a child?"

Gretchen grinned. "You'll meet my younger brother, Vince, tomorrow. I'll let him tell you how I ordered him around mercilessly when he was eight years old. He absolutely insisted that baths were dangerous to his social standing, but the threat of never seeing dessert in this lifetime convinced him that he could somehow survive a touch of soap and water."

David twisted his lips up in a bemused smile. "You withheld dessert from a boy of eight? Gutsy woman."

"Yes. Vince had lungs of steel and real staying power when he howled. I'm prepared to wade into treacherous waters when I have to."

David raised one brow.

"But I'm not stupid, David," she added quickly. "I don't take unnecessary risks."

"I'll remember that, Gretchen," he said as he stood and moved toward the door, obviously on his way back to his room. "When you and I meet on a bed next time, I'll make sure that any risks we take are very necessary ones."

The man was turning her into a feverish woman, Gretchen admitted as she slipped into the body-hugging pale sea-green dress and tugged the jacket over her shoulders late the next afternoon. One minute she was sauna-hot, the next slush-cold as she realized just how close she was getting to the edge with David.

"If it was just the sex thing, I'd be okay," she muttered. "Or even the fact that he respects me professionally." But when those two aspects of their relationship were combined with the way he seemed to almost sense her needs and her fears, and responded with caring and more restraint than any man she knew... Well, darn it, the man just scared her more than a bank robber with a wildly waving gun.

He treated her like a person who needed caring for in ways she didn't even know she needed caring for. And that affected her much too much, even though she knew it was just his way, with everyone, with every woman. Still, it touched her, made her want him in ways she didn't understand or welcome. She couldn't get away from these longings he called forth in her. The fact that he'd held back because she wanted him to, when he knew he could make her ignite with the slightest touch, confused her. He made her hurt to be with him even though she knew the danger of getting too entangled. And by danger, she was not talking about her professional standing. She just didn't want to start letting this man get too close. She *never* wanted to long for any man so much that she would give up all the things that mattered the most to her, the way her mother had done over and over.

"And there's no need to worry about that, is there?" she whispered. "He wants you. You want him, but he's been reasonable. There's no reason to think he won't play fair the rest of the time." She would get to call the shots, and she'd already made her stance clear.

Gretchen tried out a smile in the mirror and found that she looked relatively calm.

Good. She could enjoy herself as much as she wanted today without having to worry about anything else.

Gretchen's dress looked tissue-thin, her elegant shoulders were bare. When she turned and her blond hair brushed her naked flesh, David couldn't help imagining his own fingers doing the same. And right now, smiling though he might be, he was ready to arrest the next guy who looked at Gretchen as if he knew what was beneath that scrap of silk she was wearing.

The fact that he himself didn't know and might never know in spite of the comment he'd made to her upon leaving her room last night, left him raw and aching. The truth was, he wasn't going to force anything on her that she didn't feel right about. He might want to seduce her badly, he might even know that she was ready to tumble with just the slightest push, but he also knew that she was hoping against hope that she wouldn't have to deal with the complications of a physical relationship with him. Knowing that, he couldn't press her. She was right about this situation being a bit delicate and she had every right to back away if she wanted to.

That didn't mean he had to feel good about it. It only meant he had to endure. And if that was the case, he might as well endure with grace. Might as well enjoy as much of the lady's company as the situation allowed.

"You look stunningly beautiful," he whispered, brushing back her hair with his thumb and dropping a kiss on the pulse point just beneath her ear. It was early evening. For the past two hours he'd watched Gretchen walk down the aisle, stand patiently for photo after photo, assist the bride. She'd glowed and smiled, making David ache to touch her. Now he was passing through the receiving line at the reception and he'd had to watch man after man kiss Gretchen. On her cool, soft cheek. On her warm red lips. Meaningless kisses if you didn't know how men operated. David happened to know a lot about how men operated.

She smiled up at him. "The wedding went well, didn't it? Pamela was lovely."

"I'm sure she was. I didn't notice."

Staring into her eyes, his meaning was obvious. Gretchen dragged in a deep breath and continued to just stand there looking lovely. A full-bodied, chortling laugh sounded nearby.

"Looks like my big sister has finally found a man who knows how to stun her into silence."

The voice broke the spell she appeared to be under. She smiled up at David and turned to the man standing at his shoulder. "David, this is my baby brother, Vince. He's the only Neal other than me who could make it in today. Vince, this is David Hannon, my fiancé," she managed to say quite smoothly.

David turned to a handsome young man not much younger than himself. "You must be the brother Gretchen told me about. The one she threatened to withhold dessert from when he was eight?"

Vince grinned. "She's a tyrant, Hannon. I hope you can handle her. Gretch very seldom listens to anyone else's side of things."

"Humph," she said, crossing her slender arms. "I listened to you whenever that bully next door threatened you."

Vince shifted uncomfortably. "Don't remind me." He looked at David. "She's unstoppable when someone she loves is threatened, Hannon. You should know it. I distinctly remember my sister sporting a black eye for my sake that time."

Gretchen looked suddenly sad. "I'm sorry, Vince. I didn't mean to make you feel uncomfortable. I'd forgotten about the black eye. I only remembered that he was twice as tall as you and a total jerk. He stole your bicycle, if I recall."

Her brother shifted his head. He turned to David. "What's a guy to do? She forgot the black eye but remembered that Thad was twice my size. I remember that I had some real growing up to do back then. Fast, if I didn't want my sister getting beat up for my sake every other week. Having a sister like Gretch, you learned to fight your own battles or she'd get in the thick of things for you."

"Hey, he looked worse than I did when it was over," Gretchen protested.

David couldn't help chuckling at her indignant response. "I'm sure you worked him over and he got his just deserts, love. And don't worry, Vince," he told the young man. "I'm watching out for her these days."

She gave David a deadly glance.

Vince laughed. "Careful, Hannon. Her pride bruises easily."

David looked down into Gretchen's sparkling green eyes. "I'm watching out for that, too. You're lucky to have her for a sister, Vince."

"Just as long as you know how lucky you are, as well," Vince warned.

"The luckiest," David agreed. "You won't mind if I pull her out of here and keep her to myself for a few minutes before the bridal party drags her away from me, will you?"

"I was wondering if you were being a bit slow, Hannon. You seem like good prospective brother-in-law material. You chose well, Gretch. Be happy, sweetheart." He gave his sister a kiss on the cheek.

"I *am* happy, Vince. Please, don't worry about me."

But as David slipped her arm through his and escorted her away, she looked up at him. "I guess you passed. Vince seemed to relax. He's always been a little worried where I was concerned. Even though he's younger than me, he feels like I'm the headstrong one. Can you imagine?"

David laughed and lifted her up into his arms, kissing her full on the lips for everyone to see before he let her down. "I can't imagine why anyone would consider you headstrong, Gretchen. A black eye. Imagine that."

"The kid deserved it." Her tone was calm, matter-of-fact.

"I'm sure he did, but, Gretchen—"

She looked up, a question in her eyes.

"I'm sure it's a bit sexist of me, but if you ever feel like giving someone a black eye for my sake, do you think you could let me try my luck at him first?"

She smiled and patted his hand. "Of course, David, dear. Male pride. It's such a delicate thing. I'll try to be kind."

"You do that."

"As long as you don't try to fight my battles for me."

He opened his mouth to protest, then decided it would be best to not say anything. The thought of anyone touching Gretchen with the intent of hurting her filled him with such anger that he knew he couldn't promise any such thing. It wasn't because he doubted her ability. It wasn't because he really was a sexist. In fact, he was pretty sure he didn't want to know why he felt that way and pretty sure that Gretchen wouldn't want to know, either. Perhaps tonight, they shouldn't think—at all.

And so he kept her close at his side as they moved around the room and she introduced him to all the friends he hadn't yet met. He wondered what fates had linked him to this woman, this wonderful, glorious, infuriatingly self-sufficient woman.

"God, he's gorgeous, Gretchen," Pamela said for perhaps the fourth time that day. "Almost as good-looking as my Raymond. I can't believe it. Oh, you've made me so happy, sweetie. Thinking of you finally bringing home a man and to my wedding, too. It's the best present ever."

Twin tears streaked down the bride's cheeks as she hugged her friend close.

"The day's perfect now. Perfect," Pamela added. "Isn't it, Raymond?"

"The very best day of my life, love," her husband answered. "Thank you," he whispered to Gretchen and David when Pamela went to fix her makeup for the tenth time that day. "She's been worrying about you for weeks. Now she can relax and not feel guilty about getting married and 'deserting you,' as she's been saying," he admitted.

"Oh, Raymond, you should have told me she was worrying so much."

He shrugged. "What could you do to make her happy, short of getting engaged? And heaven knows, no one would get engaged for such a frivolous reason."

"I see what you mean," Gretchen said weakly as Pamela returned and her husband spirited her away.

"Relax, sweetheart," David whispered. "She's happy."

"She is, isn't she?" Gretchen agreed, smiling up at him. "And so am I. For the first time in a long time, I'm at a wedding where no one is giving me worried glances or trying to make sure I'm not alone too much. Everyone is able to relax and simply enjoy themselves, and I intend to do the same thing."

"You're a very wise and adaptable woman, Gretchen Neal," David whispered. "Have I told you that today?"

"You've never told me that," she said indignantly.

"Hmm, that can't be right. I must have. Aren't you the woman who agreed to put up with a pushy FBI agent who wormed his way onto your case?"

"I seem to remember something like that. Yes."

"And aren't you the woman who had to patiently remind me repeatedly that I couldn't play top banana all the time?"

She shook her head. "You were a fast learner."

He looked contrite. "But I'm sure you're the one who got suckered into a bet and then gamely agreed to go along with the consequences, even though she really didn't want to."

"What could I do? Fair is fair."

"And you're more than fair, Gretchen. Now, go on and do whatever it is that bridesmaids have to do at receptions and then enjoy yourself when the dancing starts. Save a slow one for me."

She touched his cheek gently. "Oh, more than one, I think. Many more." And then, as if she realized that her touch was sapping all his self-control, she blushed the palest of pinks. Her eyelids fluttered down in a way that would most certainly have surprised all those male detectives who were so used to seeing her manage dangerous situations with ease. "That is, I—we're supposed to be engaged," she ended feebly. "We would dance, wouldn't we?"

"Oh, yes, love, we would definitely dance. And more," he said, snagging her close and bending her backward over his arm as he touched his lips to hers in a brief, hard kiss. "Just in case anyone should forget that you're wearing my ring tonight," he told her.

She nodded slightly, her lips parted, her expression slightly dazed.

"Enjoy the dancing, Gretchen," he said, releasing her completely.

And she apparently did. For the next few hours Gretchen twirled. She swayed. She danced with every male that asked her. She glowed with delight, and David delighted in her unfettered enthusiasm. How could he not when the lady was in his own arms every few dances?

"For appearance's sake," she said the first time as he twirled her into the dance and later accepted a glass of wine from him to cool her off.

"Just in case anyone has any doubts," he agreed the next time she was in his arms.

"To keep everyone happy," she whispered softly the next time he fit his hand to her waist and pulled her close against his heart. Only Gretchen wasn't sure whose happiness she was worried about this time. As a bridesmaid, she'd felt obligated to dance with the guests, but her eyes had kept returning to David. It was his arms and his hands she wanted around her, his heart she wanted beating against her own. Her head was swirling. She'd probably had more wine than she should, but for now she was with David and she just didn't care.

"Let's walk outside," she said when the dance was over and she saw another young man headed her way. "I need some air and some rest. It's so warm in here."

David signaled a passing waiter to bring her another glass of wine and then thought better of it, asking the man for water instead. He'd probably had more to drink than he should. The wine had gone down too easily, unheeded as his gaze had followed her around the floor all night.

"You've been very busy," he said as they walked out into the softly lit gardens and along the length of a long blue pool with a fountain in the center.

"It's been fun," she agreed as she stopped and turned to face him. He held her glass up and she sipped the cool water, her lips brushing his fingers slightly where he grasped the delicate crystal.

His hand shook and she swayed against him.

Somehow he got rid of the glass. Somehow she was up against his heart.

"Do you have anything else you need to do tonight?" he asked.

She shook her head. "There's the bouquet, but then I don't need to be there for that this time. And anyway, Pamela will understand if I'm gone. She probably won't even notice. Her eyes haven't left Raymond all night long."

"If we leave, Gretchen," David whispered, his voice thick as he dipped the fingers of one hand into her hair, "I can't make any promises to behave like a gentleman."

He leaned and dropped a kiss on the bare skin of her shoulder. His fingers grazed the gentle slope of her breast above her dress.

She swallowed hard. "If we don't leave David, I can't promise that we won't both embarrass all the other guests."

And so he swept her close. Somehow they crossed

the ballroom, the lobby, found the elevator and closed themselves in together.

The door closed and he tugged her close, claimed her lips.

She placed her palms against his chest and pulled herself closer.

"I want us to make love," she managed to get out.

"I don't think there's any doubt that we're going to," he said as the door started to open and he glanced up, his lips still fastened to Gretchen's, just in time to see an elderly couple waiting to get in.

David reached out and pressed the Close Door button. He snatched Gretchen closer and heard the couple's soft laughter, saw the man's thumbs-up as the door locked them in again.

"Are they gone?" Gretchen whispered.

"Mmm," he agreed.

"Good." She wrenched her lips from his and began to rain kisses over his face, his chin. She touched her lips to his Adam's apple and busied her fingers with tugging open his tie.

When the door of the elevator opened this time, David scooped Gretchen into his arms and carried her down the hall. He could feel the lovely curves of her legs beneath the thin, slippery cloth of her dress.

"What are you wearing beneath this, love?" he asked, stopping long enough to kiss her lips once more, to savor the feel of her slender fingers against his scalp.

"Not much," she whispered. "Hurry, David."

He was, as she'd said, a fast learner. In a matter of seconds, David was at her door, she was leaning over in his arms to insert the key card and then, at last, they were alone in her room.

Letting her slide down the length of him, he waited until her feet found the floor. Then he reached behind her, gently gathered her wrists in his own and walked her slowly backward until her legs hit the side of the big bed. He swept his hands up her sides, his fingers resting on the low-slung straps that grazed her arms.

"Are you sure, Gretchen? Be very sure you know what you're doing. I'd do my best to turn back if we took this over the edge, but it would be much easier to do so now."

And yet his fingers shook against her skin. She closed her eyes and let the essence of him surround her. The gentle flexing of his fingertips on the straps, the knowledge that he was going to touch her at last, the fear that he would not touch her, filled her.

She opened her eyes, reached up as she gazed into the fiery depths of his green eyes. She grasped the lapels of the black suit that sat so well on his broad shoulders and she opened his jacket, shoving it off his shoulders. She slipped off the tie she'd unfastened earlier. She grasped the crisp white front of his shirt.

"David?"

"Yes, love?" Being a somewhat tall woman, there weren't many men who towered over her and made her feel small, or feminine. But when she looked up at that stunningly handsome face, she did feel feminine. The thought that countless other women had no doubt stood just this way with him rankled. He really was too good-looking for any woman's good. But she wasn't just any woman. She was herself, Gretchen Neal, and she wasn't going to wait for what she wanted.

She rose up on her toes, parted her lips and slid them across David's. Slowly. Once. Twice. Again.

He groaned, but still he didn't claim her with his arms. Her head was spinning, her breasts were aching where she'd pressed herself close against him.

"David," she whispered again.

"You know I want you, love," he said with a low moan against her lips. She could hear the slightest hesitation in his voice. And suddenly she was tired of all the questions, all the hesitation, all the good intentions and wise words she'd spoken these past couple of weeks.

The swirling longing that David called up in her was dangerous. The man himself was dangerous, and right now danger was just what she wanted. Mostly, though, she wanted David. His touch, his skin beneath her fingers, his length and weight pressing her into the depths of the bed, covering her.

"I want you, too, David. Please. Have me," she said in a frantic whisper, and with a quick wrench, she pulled on the shirt she was still holding clenched between her fingers. Buttons flew, and suddenly all that was between David's chest and her breasts was one small bit of silk that covered her.

He tightened his fingers on the slim straps of her gown and gently pulled downward, sliding her dress over her breasts and past her hips, letting the thin material slither to the ground. Only the slightest touch of silk panties covered her now.

David stared at her for long seconds. Her nipples stiffened beneath his gaze and he cupped one breast in his hand, lifted the soft round swell and kissed the sensitive bud.

She was going to faint. The sensation was simply too great as David kissed and suckled her, tugging gently on the turgid tip. When he moved to the other breast, she grasped his shoulders, digging in her fingers to keep from falling.

But he was there. Lifting her onto the bed, David shrugged out of what was left of his shirt. He lowered himself over her and claimed her lips again.

His hand stroked downward, outlining her from shoulder to breast to hip to knee. When he tugged his lips from her own, she surged upward. Nothing mattered at this moment but the magic of David's touch, and he was taking it away.

"Don't leave," she whispered, lacing her arms around him, urging him back to her.

"Not a chance," he whispered, his voice strained as he reached for his belt buckle. She stopped him with her touch, rising to her knees, rolling her head forward languorously as she freed him, exposed him and he peeled away the last layers that shielded him from her gaze.

She'd seen plenty of naked men before, of course. She was not untried, and besides, she operated daily in a man's world, a rough world. But she had never seen a man so clearly made for giving pleasure to a woman.

He was magnificently formed, his long, thick shaft standing proudly from his body.

She reached for him without thought and he surged into her hand then backed away.

"No. It has to be good. For you."

"It will be," she promised, reaching for him again.

"It will be," he promised as well, urging her back onto the bed. He removed the tiny patch of silk that still covered her and pulled her into his arms, breast to chest, thigh to thigh. Framing her face with his hands, he pleasured her with deep, long kisses.

He slid his body down the length of hers, kissing her shoulder, suckling at the tip of her breast, feathering his fingers down the inside of her thigh and then placing his lips there lightly, as well.

Pressure built within her, making her weak and helpless with longing and need.

"David, please," she said on a gasp, digging her fingers into his shoulders. "Be with me."

And he rose up above her. He gazed down at her, naked want in his eyes, and she opened to him. She welcomed him as he took care that she was safe and then entered her fully.

The feel of him filling her, joined to her, thick and long and strong, was exquisite, an ecstasy almost beyond bearing. His body came into hers, touching her over and over in the most pleasurable places.

She arched to meet him, rocked with him. Her muscles tightened around him. She grasped his biceps, shifting her hips, bringing him in deeper, and she felt the tension in his skin beneath her fingertips.

"Not yet." David choked out the words as she pulled him deeper still. "Not yet. Not alone."

And he slowed his movements, gasping for breath as he fought for control. He gained a small measure, gazing down into her eyes, his own dark with barely caged desire.

Her own need spilled over.

"Please," she whispered again. "Yes. Yes, now."

He tumbled her back. He took her down, took charge as he braced himself above her. He slid into her depths again and began the final movement. He held her gently by her wrists just above her head and thrust into her. Slowly, slowly, caressing her inside and out, turning her to melted butter. Making her hot beyond belief.

Craving climbed within her, building as he moved in her. Slow and then fast. He played her body, and she wanted—she needed—to reach the pinnacle he was urging her to. Too slowly.

"You're making me crazy," she said, biting her lip, her head lolling softly on the pillow.

"I'm past crazy, love. I'm barely hanging on." And then he reached down, just barely, expertly brushing one finger over that part of her where her body was joined to his, and she couldn't stop herself from spinning out of her body and into the sun. Hot pleasure flooded her. She heard David shout her name as he drove thick and hard into her one last time.

She fell back against the pillows and wondered if she'd ever be able to move again. And then she stopped wondering as she relaxed into drowsiness and let her suddenly leaden limbs rest.

The clock ticked. The time passed.

After long moments of simply waiting for thought and steady heartbeat and even breathing to return, David gathered her close in his arms. He touched his lips to her hair.

She remembered wishing that she could always feel this wonderful, this glowing. She had never lost herself so completely. She had felt so storm-tossed and yet still safe. Surely she had been right to give in to this.

Ten

"No." The word sounded in her head so clearly that Gretchen could almost have sworn that she had spoken it out loud. This morning her head was only slightly fuzzy, slightly pained, but the sense that something was very wrong was excessively strong. And she knew just what that something wrong was. She'd thrown common sense out the window last night.

Turning her head to the side, she looked right into David's eyes. He wasn't smiling.

She sat bolt upright in bed, clutching the sheet to her.

"It seems—" She couldn't quite get the words out of her mouth without needing to close her eyes, without stumbling.

"Gretchen." One word, a deep command in his voice. "Look at me."

She did. His eyes were dark green, worried.

"It seems we made a mistake," she finished.

"Like hell we did."

"I probably had too much to drink. Maybe you did, too," she whispered. "Otherwise—"

"We didn't have too much to drink. And we knew this was going to happen someday, Gretchen. We were going to make love one way or another."

She froze, spearing him with a look. "You would have forced me?"

Dark anger flooded his eyes. He sat up and reached out for her. She scooted back against the headboard.

"Damn it, Gretchen. You know there would have been no force."

"You're right." She couldn't keep the coldness from her voice. "I seem to have a surprising lack of control where you're concerned."

"Which really ticks you off, doesn't it?"

She blew out a long breath. "You don't understand, David." Her voice softened.

He rose up on his palms, leaning over her. "I understand. You value your privacy. You don't want anyone breaking down those barriers you put up, and you don't trust me to honor those barriers. You don't trust me not to push."

She opened her mouth to answer, then closed it again. Because the truth was much more frightening than that, as far as she was concerned. It wasn't that she didn't trust him not to push. She didn't trust herself not to give in. This man had the power to make her feel too much. And feeling more than she should could only lead her down paths she would regret and down paths he would regret, as well. David wanted her, but he was a man who chose to be a loner and who was here on a temporary assignment. In no time at all, he would be returning to his own world and she would stay in hers.

"We can't do this again, David," she whispered. "It was a mistake."

"All right, then," he suddenly agreed, his voice low and calm. "It was a mistake."

He meant that, David thought as they both went about the business of getting ready to leave. Making love to Gretchen *had* been a mistake, because back in his room, imagining her in the shower with warm fingers of water caressing her body, he already wanted her again. He was losing control where this woman was concerned. He wanted her way too much, too often. She seldom left his thoughts for long. And yet there was no future here. She wanted a life alone. He could understand that. He'd been a loner too long not to know the lure of that life. She was a woman who had given and given all her life, a woman who'd grown up in a big family and had had responsibility thrust on her all during the years when she should have been carefree and unencumbered by burdens.

He wanted to tell her that he would never take advantage of her that way and yet, he couldn't promise that. Because right now he wanted to ask a great deal of her. At this point in time, he couldn't be trusted from one minute to the next. Not where Gretchen was concerned. His feelings were intensifying and that was dangerous. To her and to him. Growing up sickly, cut off from children his own age, he'd wanted so much. Too much. That need to belong, that longing to be a part of a world that was closed to him, had nearly driven him mad as a child. Until he'd learned to submerge those needs, to depend only on himself. And now he was starting to feel that intense longing again.

Gretchen was right. Getting too involved with her would be a mistake. He'd do his best to keep things light and easy from now on. As for desire, that could be managed, too. He'd always been able to handle it before.

The only thing he couldn't manage was returning things to the way they'd been before they'd made love. No matter how much they both wanted to deny it, that intimacy couldn't be forgotten. It would change things. He wasn't sure how or by how much, but there would definitely be a difference. There was just no road back to yesterday.

"Okay, next verse," Gretchen said with a laugh the following Monday. David watched her as she sat cross-legged and hugging a guitar in the center of a circle of giggling children, leading them through a song she had made up to teach them safety rules. The song was silly, but the rules were very real and David was sure that the children would remember them much better than they would have if Gretchen had simply written a list on the chalkboard.

At a pause in the song, a solemn little red-haired girl tugged on Gretchen's sleeve and when Gretchen smiled down at her, the little girl leaned close. "Agent Hannon isn't singing," the child whispered a bit too loudly. "He looks mad."

Gretchen looked up from her position on the floor to where David was lounging easily against the wall, his arms crossed.

"He does look a bit…tense," she teased.

David couldn't help smiling then. And why not? Gretchen, after all, had been treating him to her own smile all morning, convinced that she had finally tamed him by bringing him in as a "classroom exhibit." She was looking absolutely beautiful in pale gray, her hair slightly mussed after a long session with the children. And yes, David acknowledged, he supposed he had looked a bit angry just a moment ago. He had been frowning, at least.

Because that smile of Gretchen's was so damned tempting. And also because the lady was clearly, totally in her element with these children and yet he knew she had decided not to get married and have any of her own. It was a crime, if anything was. He'd been mulling over that fact, and regretting it.

But then, who was he to challenge the lady's choices when she'd obviously made them carefully? She didn't think she was up to making the sacrifices that marriage would entail. Well, who was he to talk when he was pretty darn sure that he wasn't a prime choice for marriage, either?

And why was he frowning and upsetting innocent children when absolutely none of this was their fault?

David gave a deep inner sigh. He pulled his thoughts back into place, back where they should be. He turned to the little girl and gave her a wink and a grin.

"Sorry for looking like a thundercloud. I was just sulking because you weren't paying any attention to me," he teased. "Detective Neal looks like she's having all the fun."

The little girl giggled as Gretchen rolled her eyes.

"Well, then, Agent Hannon," Gretchen said, patting the floor beside her. "Why don't you come over here and help us out? We could use a baritone."

"She only keeps me around for my voice," he said

in a mock sorrowful tone as he took a place in the circle of children.

"And so you can help her fight the bad guys," one little boy said. "That's what you do, isn't it?"

David turned to the wide gray eyes of the little boy who was looking right and left, first at Gretchen, then at himself. He was rocking and fidgeting, clearly excited. "I'd like to fight those guys, too," he confided.

David knew just how the skinny little guy who was way too small to fight anyone bigger than a watermelon felt. He'd been that child once a long time ago. But he also knew things he hadn't known then.

"My job is to protect, yes, but it's more important to prevent," he confided. "Listen to the words of the song Gretchen is singing. All those things are designed to keep you as safe as possible so the bad guys won't have a chance. That's fighting them in your own way."

The little boy narrowed his eyes and shook his head. "Aw, we hear those rules all the time. They don't do anything. And it's the same old stuff every year."

"Jamie," Gretchen drawled, her voice soft. "I'm sorry you feel that way, hon, but—" David reached out and touched her hand, almost imperceptibly, stopping her midword.

"Same old stuff," he agreed gruffly, trying not to notice the quick wounded look in Gretchen's eyes. "Wonder why we keep nagging you about the same old things all the time. Day in. Day out. Year in. Year out." David gave a loud yawn, covering his hand and pretended to fall asleep slumping down sideways against Gretchen.

"David," she yelped as the children laughed.

He opened his eyes and gave her a big grin as he sat up. "Why *do* we keep coming here with the same thing year after year?" he asked. "Is it because we've forgotten what we said the year before? Is it because we just don't know any better?"

"But Gretchen does it differently every time she comes here," another little boy said, bunching his forehead and his fists. "Last visit she put on a play and before that we went on a field trip around town looking for all the ways we could make ourselves safer. She doesn't make it all the same even if the rules don't change." And he would clearly like to punch David in the nose for seemingly criticizing his beloved Gretchen. David could have hugged the boy just for that.

"Do you think that's maybe because she knows that it's not always the same? Ever. The rules don't change, but the situations do. Like the rules about strangers. We ask you not to talk to strangers and sometimes we give examples."

"Like a man offers you candy," the little red-haired girl said.

"Exactly, sweet stuff," David said. "But what if the stranger told you that he needed you to come help him find his lost puppy?"

"You run away just the same as the man with the candy," she said firmly.

"I love the fact that you know that," he confided. "Or what if he told you his little girl was sick and he needed your help."

"Oh," a little girl with big blue eyes said. "We could help then, couldn't we?"

A freckle-faced boy groaned. "Elly, no. If his little girl was sick, he should be getting a grown-up to help."

The little girl turned pink and tried to slide backward. David smiled at her. "You've got a heart that glows with goodness, Elly. I'm glad you'd want to help, but the point is, and the rule is, that if a stranger needs help, he goes to the nearest grown-up. And if someone asks you for help, you run away to the nearest grown-up. If the person really needs help, they'll get it that way. And if they were just trying to harm you in some way, an adult can help keep you safe."

He smiled at the little girl again.

"He looks very nice when he smiles, doesn't he, Gretchen?" the little red-haired girl asked.

David raised one brow and grinned at Gretchen who was looking slightly flustered. Then Gretchen obviously collected herself. She raised one delicate brow and smiled teasingly.

"He's a looker, all right, Mary Kate."

All the boys groaned.

The little boy who'd wanted to fight the bad guys stared at David. "So that's why she keeps repeating the same rules every year. So we see that they stay the same even if everything else changes?"

"That's part of the reason," David agreed. "And also just so you don't forget. So you know them so well that you can remember them without thinking. For those times when your brain short-circuits."

The little boy looked confused. "I don't get it."

Elly gave him a patient, motherly look. "You know, Jamie, like when you know you're not supposed to pet a strange dog but then one comes up to you and it's just so-oo happy to see you. Don't you remember when you and I saw that lady walking her dog this summer and you—"

Jamie slumped down a bit lower. "Okay, I remember. I get it now. Sometimes we do get so excited we forget the rules."

The little boy looked slightly defeated. He had obviously wanted, maybe even needed, to win something, David decided.

"We all forget sometimes, Jamie," he confided. "Even grown-ups. Even grown-ups who aren't ever supposed to make mistakes make them."

The boy looked up. "Not you?" he asked incredulously.

David tried to look abashed. "Me, too," he said. "Especially where dogs are concerned. You can ask Detective Neal."

The lady nodded sadly. "He has a weakness," she confessed.

"I'm working on it," David said, knowing that he really did have a weakness, but it wasn't just for exuberant, irresistible puppies. He seemed to have developed an even greater weakness, for one lovely, courageous female detective who had a soft spot for kids.

"You come back next year," the little red-haired girl told him, patting him on the hand with her own small one. "Gretchen will keep reminding you and one day you'll get past your weakness."

He hoped so, David thought as he and Gretchen said goodbye to the children later and left the school behind. He hoped he would be able to get past this abominable weakness. He'd gotten past his physical weakness as a child. Surely he'd be able to overcome his weakness for this woman, as well.

"I don't know how I missed this, Gretch," the young woman at the lab was saying the next afternoon. "That shirt was gone over very thoroughly. Or so I thought."

Gretchen stared down at the small slip of paper Reba Peyton was indicating.

"It was in his pocket?"

"Wadded up tiny and shoved down deep," Reba replied. "That's the only excuse I can give. That it was overlooked and once it had been overlooked, the shirt hadn't been moved."

Nodding, Gretchen studied the cryptic note. Very short. Very simple. Not much to it at all, and yet...

"Thanks, Reba. This changes a few things. Maybe."

And maybe it changed nothing, she conceded as she drove away. But at least it gave her some direction, something to do. At least she wasn't just twiddling her fingers and thinking of David Hannon, acting like a woman without a brain.

She considered heading back to the station, but that would have been out of the way, and besides, David had mentioned that he had a few calls to make regarding a case he still had open in Atlanta. Surely he wouldn't want her to interrupt him. This was, after all, just a preliminary questioning. Nothing too involved. Nothing she needed to consult with anyone on.

"Should be a piece of cake compared to some things I've done lately," she conceded, but she refused to dwell on what those things had been. Instead she concentrated on making sure that Lyle Brooks's car was in the parking lot outside the expensive boxy condos where he lived.

The car was there.

Good. Finally something positive was happening.

The housekeeper that had led her into Lyle's office quietly slipped away, clicking the door shut behind her.

Lyle looked up from some scribbling he was doing.

"Detective Neal?" he said with some surprise. "Esther told me it was you, but I thought maybe she'd got it wrong."

"No, she wasn't wrong," Gretchen said in an even tone. Brooks was a small man, with dark hair and dark vacant eyes. His expensive suit fit him well but didn't enhance his image. It was more like a costly wrapping on a slightly used present. The thought rose up. She brushed it aside. No fair prejudging the man even though he always made her uncomfortable and slightly tense.

"Mr. Brooks," she said as he tried out a smile that moved his mouth but otherwise made no difference in his appearance. "I have a few questions about Peter Cook and I'd like to ask your cooperation on several matters."

"Of course, Ms. Neal," he said, leaving off her title. "What can I do for you?"

"You can tell me why you wrote Peter Cook a note asking him to meet you at the site at ten o'clock the night he fell."

He shrugged. "No mystery here, Ms. Neal. Peter and I were close. He wanted to see this project finished as much as I do. I often included him in my planning sessions, and I often made my plans for the next day after hours. It simplifies things, ensures that all of the day's problems have been put away before we move on to the next day's concerns. Anything else?"

"Yes, Mr. Brooks. How long exactly did you and Peter spend together that night?"

She gazed down at him unblinkingly. He still smiled up at her, but she noticed that he'd flattened the fingers of one hand against the desk's edge. As if he wanted to keep from making a fist. Or curling his fingers around her neck. Not exactly a novel response. She'd seen it before, from the guilty and from the innocent. There were plenty of people, herself included, who didn't enjoy having their actions questioned. She tried to remind herself that this wasn't something she hadn't experienced before, although it did feel different somehow. Off kilter. But then, she had been rather off kilter lately and her reactions hadn't had much to do with her work.

"Mr. Brooks?" she prompted.

He shook his head. "It was a very brief meeting. We were simply discussing the next day's continued excavation. We went over the plans and then I left to go to the country club. I assure you Peter was alive and happy when last I saw him. The work was going well. I'm afraid I don't know anything about what happened to him after I departed, Ms. Neal. I'm sorry."

Yes, she was, too.

"I understand that you can only tell me what you know, Mr. Brooks," she agreed. "I hope that *you'll* understand when I tell you that we'd like to obtain some hair, skin and blood samples from you."

The silence was enormous. Then the man slowly smiled. "Of course, Ms. Neal. I want to find out what happened and to help all of us to move on in time."

She tilted her head in agreement. "Then we have the same goals, Mr. Brooks."

"And what would life be like without goals?" he said with a cheerful smile. "Don't worry, Ms. Neal. You'll have your samples. I know you're just doing your job."

He rose as she thanked him. He held out his hand, and she had no choice but to take it. Truthfully, she wasn't sure why she would want to hesitate. His explanation seemed plausible, given the situation. She was probably just a bit jumpy. She'd been much too jumpy lately. That really wasn't Lyle Brooks's fault.

But as she left Lyle's condo, she had an itchy need to look back over her shoulder.

The lady cop had very bad timing, Lyle Brooks thought after she left. His day had not gone well. He'd spent long hours trying to convince the leaders at the reservation that the Kincaid property that had been set aside for the resort/casino was the wrong piece of property. Two bodies. The land was undoubtedly bad luck. Cursed, one might even say, if a person believed in such things.

He believed in curses, although not this one that he'd conveniently invented. His whole life he'd been cursed, but now he had a chance. All he had to do was convince those people, those undeserving partners of his, to use *his* property that skirted the reservation in lieu of the current tract of land they'd chosen. They'd be happy, he'd still be in charge, and no one would go nosing around those sapphires.

Except for him, of course. He was the only one who even knew they existed now that Peter was gone. Convincing the Cheyenne to move to a different location was the perfect solution.

If only they'd listen.

But they weren't listening. Something about destiny and dreams and this land being the perfect land.

Lyle Brooks let out a growl. His fist came down

hard on the desk, sending paper clips and pens and an expensive ashtray flying.

He was just going to have to convince them. He didn't want anyone nosing around that land and discovering those sapphires that, right now, were his for the taking.

And he didn't want Detective Neal nosing around his business, either. Not that she could prove a thing. He'd been careful. No prints. Not even much of a touch to send Cook over the edge. Peter hadn't expected to be pushed. It had been easy to remove him as an obstacle.

He intended for it to be easy to remove every other obstacle or anyone who tried to cross him, as well. Lyle flicked a paper clip with his finger. A short, simple painless movement, but the paper clip flew through the air and fell to the ground. If it had been something breakable, it would have broken.

His laugh was low and strong as he thought how easy things were going to be.

Eleven

Gretchen opened the door a few hours later and unfastened the chain when she saw that it was David standing there. She gave him a smile.

"You don't have to keep coming to walk Goliath," she said when the little dog came running.

David absentmindedly reached down and gave the dog a quick pat, but he turned his attention back to Gretchen immediately. He wasn't smiling.

"I didn't come to see Goliath," he said.

He still wasn't smiling. His eyes were dark green and fierce. His face was set in sharp lines. He rested one hand on the door frame, making him seem even taller and broader of shoulder than usual.

Gretchen looked up at him and she wanted nothing more than to slide her hands up to frame that starkly handsome face of his and to brush her thumbs across his lips. She wanted to press her lips to his and see if the light came back into his eyes. A slight tremor ran through her at just the thought, at just how much this man made her lose every drop of common sense she possessed.

"Come inside, anyway," she said softly, stepping back to let him in.

He stepped in, letting the door fall shut behind him and then he kept coming.

"Gretchen," he said on a growl, moving into her space, gripping her arms lightly but firmly so that she was forced to look up at him. "What in hell were you doing today, lady?"

She looked down at where he held her, trying to make her eyes disdainful and cool, to ignore the fact that his touch fired through her and made her want to move closer.

"I was working," she said, her voice coming out too soft for her own satisfaction. "I was doing my job. What are you talking about?"

He shuffled forward one step, bringing his chest almost up against her own, moving his hands up to her shoulders, crowding her, a pained look on his face.

"You know what I'm talking about."

She did.

"I was doing my job, Hannon."

"You went to see Lyle Brooks. You went alone."

She placed her hands on his chest and pushed lightly. He backed off.

"I wasn't making an arrest, David. I was only asking a few questions. Standard stuff. Nothing to get excited about. I've done it a million times."

"Not with Lyle Brooks. I don't like the man."

"Neither do I, and he's being way too complacent for a man who has a reputation for impatience. The excavation of his resort has been held up and he's not screaming loudly enough, I think."

"I think you're right. And when a man starts acting out of character, he isn't a safe prospect."

He stared at her pointedly, the heat and frustration and anger rolling off him in long, slow waves. His jaw was like cold steel, his eyes like twin green flames.

Gretchen let out a sigh. She gave a gentle shrug, shaking her head. "David, I didn't need to tell you," she emphasized. "You were otherwise occupied. Don't try to tell me I wasn't doing my job right."

"You weren't."

Her chin came up. "That's unfair. Furthermore, it's not true. If you're going to make those kinds of accusations, Hannon, you'd darn well better have a good reason for making them. I followed the letter of the law."

"I'm not talking about the law this time, Gretchen. I'm talking about common sense. You know that guy is slime. Even if he didn't commit a crime here, he's not the kind of man you go up to alone and ask for evidence that indicates you might be suspicious of him."

"I do."

"Not when you have a partner, you don't. Let's try for a little trust here."

"All right, let's try for a little trust," she agreed. "If you had trusted me to do my job, you wouldn't have insisted on being allowed on this case. So who doesn't trust whom now? And for the record, David, my actions today had nothing to do with my lack of trust in you. You were working on something else. And it seems to me that I've trusted you quite a bit. I've shared my work with you. I've taken you to meet my friends when I've never done that with anyone else. But you just keep—"

She took a long deep breath and closed her eyes.

"But what, Gretchen? What is it I've done to upset you?"

Gretchen leaned back and looked up into his eyes. "You keep pushing. You keep making me uncomfortable." She breathed in again and the small action brought her chest up against his.

His eyes turned dark and slumberous. "I make you uncomfortable, do I? In what way would that be?"

But her eyelids drifted down. She didn't want to give him his answer, and besides, darn it, he knew what way he made her uncomfortable. He knew it too well, she could tell, by the way his thumbs were rubbing slow circles upon the skin of her upper arms.

He leaned in closer, dragging her against him. "In this way?" he whispered, covering her lips with his own, sweeping her against him, her hips against his so that she could feel every angry inch of him. So that she could know that she made him uncomfortable, as well.

"No. In this way," she said when they came back up for air, and she plunged her fingers into his hair. She rose on her toes and molded her body to his, sliding up against him as she took the heat of his mouth.

Her lips chained him to her, held him still, made him moan. He was hers for the moment. He stood there and let her kiss him, his body tense and taut.

And then he moved. His mouth roved over hers, lightly at first, exploring. He shifted, lingering longer over each taste of her. The kiss turned dark and deep and hungry. He fed on her, taking her under time and time again. His hands claimed her shoulders, his fingertips teased her breasts.

She arched into him and pushed against his touch.

"Do that again. Please," she said, and he popped the top three buttons of her blouse, freeing the lace and pale skin that lay beneath.

"Touch me," he whispered, his voice ragged as his lips came down on hers once more and his fingers found the clasp of her bra and released her.

When his thumb grazed her nipple, she tore her lips from his, grasped the collar of his shirt and pulled on the cloth in one quick, jagged move, baring the golden muscles that lay beneath. Her palms came up against his chest and she lightly pushed, waltzing him backward across the carpeting toward the couch.

"No," he said, covering both her hands with one of his own to stop her. He only waited for her to pause before he scooped her into his arms.

"No?" Gretchen looked into his eyes, her own vision dull and glazed.

"Not the couch. We need room," he whispered, whisking her into the bedroom, striding the width of the floor and falling with her onto the bed.

"Room. Yes," she agreed, rolling from beneath him as she climbed to her knees and slid his shirt off his shoulders. She pushed, and he lay back against the pillows. Her lips found the small male nipple she was seeking.

A long, low breath slid from between David's lips as he let her lead the way. Gretchen leaned over him, her blouse curtaining his torso as she rose up to study him. He was beautiful, golden and hers for the moment, and she intended to feast.

Her tongue swirled against his skin. The flavor of him was a joy to the senses. She kissed her way over the tight muscles in his chest, dipping down to savor that washboard stomach. Finding his belt with her hand, she quickly flicked open the buckle and reached for the snap on his jeans. Her fingers slid beneath the waistband and she heard the slow hiss of his breath.

"Better to wait on that, love," he said on a gasp. "I want to make this last. At least a little bit longer." And without knowing exactly how he did it, Gretchen found herself in David's arms, sliding beneath him. With a few efficient movements, he tossed away her blouse, sent her bra sailing and removed her slacks, leaving only her ice-blue satin panties.

His smile was wolfish as he reclaimed the dominant role. "You are the most delicious, beautiful thing I've ever seen," he whispered, his warm breath teasing her skin as he nuzzled her hair aside and began to lightly nibble his way beneath her ear, down the exquisitely sensitive column of her neck.

"Soft," he murmured, dropping the lightest of kisses on the rounded slope of her breast.

"Firm," he whispered, his lips just catching the tip of her breast, tugging, tightening, then taking her into his mouth when she cried out at the heavenly sensation.

She thought she would go mad when he pulled away and gazed down at her. But he only paused to brush her lips lightly with his own before he turned his attention to her other breast, rolling the nipple between his lips, then suckling her gently.

A burgeoning need heated her, as sensation spiraled in her breasts and between her legs. She pressed her thighs together as David stroked her body, leading her, lifting her to heights of want she had never known.

"Gretchen, love." The words were strained with tension and Gretchen opened her eyes to look up at the man who controlled her every reaction at this moment. His eyes were dark with need and wonder and reverence. The fingers he touched to her lips shook. She knew that he was holding back everything that was coiled tightly within him. A light sheen of perspiration covered his magnificent chest. He needed her touch, needed release and yet when she reached for him again, to free him from the constraints of his remaining clothing, he closed his eyes and shook his head.

"David?"

He took a deep breath, opened his eyes and smiled at her slightly as he kissed his fingers, dampening them and then lightly touching the tip of her breast again. His light touch against her distended nipple sent her whole body bowing upward.

She called out his name again and he slid his hand down her body, parting her thighs as he reached beneath that scrap of silk and found the center of her, his fingers slipping in deep to stroke and tease.

And she flew apart on a broken cry. She lost herself to immeasurable pleasure. She touched the sun, the edge of the rainbow, and the deepest depths of the ocean in the same moment.

And David held her as she gave in to ecstasy.

When the tremors had finally subsided just slightly, she opened her eyes and looked up into his. He cupped her jaw, caressed her cheek.

"Well, I see I'm still here on earth, after all," she said, her voice weakened but still filled with the glow of satisfaction.

"Not for long," he whispered with a smile. "We're only halfway to heaven, angel."

"I was sure I was almost there."

"Soon," he promised, sitting up to skim his jeans down his legs and stepping out of his briefs. His body was long and lean and fully aroused.

Gretchen trembled as he moved back to the bed and gazed down at her, impatient desire written in every detail of his body.

"Maybe I was only halfway to heaven," she agreed brokenly, pushing up on her elbows, rising to her knees.

"Gretchen," he warned as she reached out for him, her small slender fingertips lightly tracking down his body from shoulder to waist to hips.

"This time I lead, partner," she whispered, kissing his beautiful chest, sliding her fingers over his warm male skin, lightly stroking all of him. He was hard and long and strong and she wanted him.

"A trip to heaven for two," she whispered. "Now."

And she pushed him back and slid onto the length of him.

"Now, sweetheart," he said with a low growl as she mated her body to his.

Rising and falling, she pleasured them both, loving the feel of his skin beneath her fingers, of her own body closing around his over and over again.

"Gretchen, come here," he said as he rolled over and took control again. He took her hands lightly in his own, holding them gently over her head as he thrust into her slowly. So slowly, pulling himself out and then slipping in deep. Touching her in places she had never been touched.

Her pleasure rose and rose. David slid into her depths again and again. The corded muscles on his arms stood out as he held back.

"Heaven." He choked the words out.

"David. Oh, yes. Heaven." The words flew from her as she reached the peak and he tumbled after her with a satisfied groan.

The world went silent except for the sound of their breathing. Gretchen lay beneath the man who had stolen her will, sapped her strength and shared her soul for the last length of time. He shifted, taking the weight of his body away and she felt the loss.

The very thought sent a tiny shaft of fear echoing through her. The need to pull him close again, to fold herself into the haven of his body was almost overwhelming. And not just for the pleasure he could provide her, she knew all too well. It was the man himself who pulled at her emotions so deeply. The yearning to reach out for him nearly cut her breath off. The thought that she could ever want that badly was like a straitjacket, binding her, cutting off her choices and the freedom she'd worked for all her life. Especially since this man wasn't known for staying in one place with one woman for very long. How could she have allowed this to happen? She couldn't, Gretchen told herself. With the greatest effort, she edged away from the sensation, pushing it into the deepest recesses of her mind.

Groggily, she pushed up to her knees, brushing her hair from her eyes.

Deep emerald eyes studied her. A mouth that could kill a woman with pleasure lifted into a smile. She reached out to touch, then pulled her hand back.

"Hi, angel," he said, rising to join her, his height bringing him up above her. He reached out, cupped her cheek and gently kissed her before she had time to think or to stop him. "Thank you for the sweetest hour I think I've ever spent."

For just a second her eyes softened, but David didn't miss the shades that slipped over those sea-green windows immediately after. She was already distancing herself from him, already pulling away. The thought made him angry, and he didn't want to be angry with her anymore today. True, it was his anger that had made him reckless and blind and brought him here with her to the edge of bliss, but it wasn't anger they'd shared here on this bed.

And he knew now that he wanted to share something very special with Gretchen Neal. For however far it went, he wanted them to go together. He wanted her to trust him for more than a few minutes of ultimate ecstasy.

"Don't do that," he whispered, holding her still when she started to pull away, to slip backward off the bed, out of his arms, and, he was sure, as far away from him emotionally and physically as she could go.

"Don't do what?" She tossed her chin up, halting her backward movement, halting her physical retreat but not coming closer in any emotional sense.

"Damn it, Gretchen," he said, his voice hoarse and a bit hard. "Don't act as if you don't want to be near me when we just shared something pretty spectacular. Don't pretend it didn't happen."

She took a deep breath, licked her lips nervously. And that slight vulnerable motion, the scared-puppy look in her eyes nearly did him in.

"I'm not. I won't. It was beyond pretty spectacular," she said, her voice so low he could barely hear her. "It was totally spectacular. Wonderful, in fact." Her lashes dipped low, hiding her lovely eyes from him.

"It wasn't just sex," he insisted, curving his palm around her arm, stroking lightly with his thumb. "It went beyond the moment."

She didn't answer, but he felt the tension in her body, as though she was holding in her breath, trying not to feel or react.

"Gretchen? Don't tell me you're regretting this time with me."

She breathed in deeply. "No," she said slowly, firmly, placing her hands lightly on his chest, looking him full in the eyes. "I don't regret making love with you, David."

"You're afraid I'll ask for more."

"Do you have more to give?"

He studied her for long seconds, wanting to say yes but having no basis for those words.

"I don't know how much I have to give," he finally admitted, "but I know we can share more than a few hours of passion. I want more than that with you."

She opened her mouth as if to speak and leaned in close. Then she tamed her parted lips. She kissed him softly on the mouth.

"I can't think beyond the day, David. I don't want to think of the future. Just today. Just now."

And though her words were as soft as her body, they sliced right through him, wounding him in ways he hadn't realized he could be wounded. But her eyes…oh, her eyes were large and wide and completely vulnerable. Because he was pushing her when he had no right to push, asking for answers he'd learned in the past he couldn't give himself.

David pulled her close. He pressed her head to his chest, running his palm over the silk of her hair.

"You're right, Gretchen, sweetheart. Just today. Just now."

And she twined her arms around him.

He entered her slowly. He savored the moment as the

world fell away and the lady gave him her all, her body, her pleasure, her world. Her today.

And he took.

Because today was all that either of them could promise.

The workday had barely begun when Gretchen looked up to see Storm Hunter talking to Rafe Rawlings two days later. It wasn't the only time since that first fateful day that he'd come into the station. He seemed to have a need to check up on the progress of the investigation—or a desire to make a point. He wasn't going to simply sit around with his thumbs in his belt loops while the law took its sweet time on this case.

At that moment he turned to the side and caught sight of her. His dark eyes narrowed. He raised his proud chin and for a second Gretchen thought she knew what Raven must have looked like when Jeremiah had insulted him by insinuating that he wasn't good enough for his sister.

But she wasn't Jeremiah, Gretchen reminded herself, and there was no question that Storm was here to ask about her case. She rose and headed his way. She was just a few feet away from him when his lips turned up just slightly in a cold, knowing smile.

She turned to see what he was looking at and gazed straight into David's eyes as he came in the door.

"Your boyfriend's here, Detective," Storm said softly. She wanted to squirm. She wanted to deny. She wanted to proudly proclaim that it was true. Instead she did none of those things. She simply raised one brow.

"That's old territory, and we've already covered it, Storm," she said quietly.

"You deny that the Neal-Kincaid ties are growing tighter? You've been seen together after hours. A great deal," he said with a slow nod of his head.

"What can I do for you, Storm?" she asked, her voice calm and devoid of the emotion that churned inside of her.

He shook his head. "I don't think you can do a thing for me, Detective. If you could, you already would have."

"We'll do all we can to solve Raven's case," she said once again.

"Or I'll solve it myself," he said quietly, stepping around her and moving down the aisle, headed toward the door.

"What was that all about?" David asked as he reached her elbow. "You okay?" he asked.

She nodded and turned to Rafe. "As to what it's all about, I can't completely say. What did he come for, Rafe?"

The man shook his head. "Same thing he always does, Gretchen. Information. I've told him a thousand times that the case is yours."

"He doesn't want to hear that," she told Rafe and David. "He wants to hear that we have some answers. Unfortunately, we don't have any yet. There's just not enough hard evidence. I hope we find something soon."

"So do I," David said. "I just talked to Phil. I have a case that looks like it may need my attention real soon, and it seems my time here is running out. I'm expected back in Atlanta in a week."

Gretchen knew that she should have felt glad to hear that news. When he'd first arrived she would have cheered at the prospect of getting rid of him. Now all she could think was that a week wasn't nearly enough time. Not for this case, and not for herself. The fact that she felt that way was enough to prove to her that it was, in fact, a good thing that David was going back home. A very good thing.

If she didn't get in any deeper, she'd be just fine.

Twelve

It was the next evening and Gretchen was trying very hard to convince herself that the book on her lap interested her. It should have, but she was preoccupied, too conscious of the passing of time, too aware of the man sitting beside her on her old blue-and-white-plaid sofa. And that just wouldn't do. She had to stay focused on what really mattered, on the things she could control. On her work.

She intended to do that even though up until this moment she and David had simply been sharing each other's company. They hadn't engaged in work at all. How had that happened? Why had she invited him to dinner?

Gretchen didn't know—or maybe she just didn't want to examine those motives too closely. Instead she cleared her throat and looked up at the man who raised his beautiful eyes from the newspaper he'd been studying.

"What would you do if you were in love with a woman who also happened to be carrying your child and her brother tried to do everything in his power to get you to leave her?" she suddenly said.

David sucked in a breath, and she wished that she hadn't used the word "love."

"You're trying to retrace Raven's last day again?" he finally asked.

She felt her muscles relaxing, glad that they were back to the clear-cut parameters of work. "What else is there to do? We've got nothing else to go on."

"I know. I've been doing the same thing, and I'll tell you what I'd do. If I loved a woman, truly, desperately loved her, and someone was effectively trying to keep her from me, I might do anything."

The words were forced from David's lips as though he struggled with the very concept of love. Gretchen knew how he felt. She definitely didn't want to think about love—or to think about David loving one particular woman.

"Maybe I'd just pace and snarl at everyone," he continued. "I've talked to people who saw Raven in those last few days, and he apparently did a lot of that. I might get in a few arguments. He did that, too. And yes, most likely I'd confront the man who was hiding her from me. That's the one thing we don't know about. There's no record of Jeremiah and Raven meeting after Jeremiah gave Raven the money." He stared at her long and hard. "But that doesn't mean it didn't happen. Those two men were first-class enemies. Raven had good reason to hate Jeremiah and anything could have happened between them."

Gretchen let out a sigh. "And maybe nothing did.

Maybe Raven, in his anger and grief, picked a fight with someone who decided to shoot him. Maybe there were other circumstances we don't know anything about. We just don't know enough."

"We know that Jeremiah had several guns that could have been the murder weapon, but then, we haven't been able to conclusively link those weapons to that bullet."

"So we're just going around in circles again, David," she said, rising to her feet.

"Not exactly," he said with a soft murmur, standing and taking her hands in his own. "We've talked to a lot of people in the past few weeks. We've learned something of both of these men. We know that there was a lot of powerful emotion between these men, and those kinds of things get noted, get stored away in people's memory banks along with other snippets of information that seemed to be lost over time. Maybe in time if we keep hammering away, those events will resurface in someone's memory and we'll know a little more about what happened between Jeremiah and Raven."

She tried out a smile. "Maybe in time?"

He pulled her to him with a gentle tug. "I was…presumptuous in coming here to help you with your investigation. You never really needed my help, after all. You'll find your answers."

Gretchen dredged up a smile from somewhere. "Don't underestimate yourself, Hannon. You have a way of getting people to open up. Women, especially, seem to remember things, little bits of conversations, that they had forgotten until you start jogging their memory. Wasn't it Lily Mae who, when you were questioning her the other day, finally remembered Raven telling her that he never gave up what was his?"

David smiled. "I believe the lady was trying to make a point. She was digging for information on you and me, trying to see if I felt the same way about what was mine."

Gretchen's eyes widened. She sucked in her breath. "Well, nevertheless, I—"

"I'll miss you when we're done," he said, pulling her to him, kissing her lips. "We're not done yet, Gretchen."

She let out the air she'd been holding in, studied the man in front of her, and realized just how lucky she'd been to have him show up in this town. Professionally and personally. "No, we're not done yet," she whispered, feathering her lips across his, opening to invite him inside.

But apparently they were done for now. The doorbell rang at that instant, and David growled low in his throat as he let her go.

When she opened the door, her friend Karen was standing there. The woman let out a squeal.

"Gretch," she said, throwing her arms around Gretchen. "Guess what? I was on my way to Helena to visit my mother and my car nearly ran out of gas just outside Whitehorn. I figured it had to be fate, and besides, I don't see you nearly enough. It seemed like too good an opportunity to stop and say hello in person. I tried to call you earlier but you must have been out on a case or something. So, here I am."

The words came out on a long breathless rush the way they always did with Karen. Her face was glowing and pretty with enthusiasm and Gretchen couldn't keep from smiling in spite of her disappointment at having her time with David cut short. She hugged her friend and stepped back from the doorway.

"Come on in," she said. "You remember David?"

Karen's eyes were like blue stars. "Gretch, how could any woman with eyeballs in her head forget David? The man is better than double chocolate pudding topped with whipped cream and sprinkles," she said, giving David a sisterly hug. "I just got finished telling his aunt so myself. I'm staying at the Big Sky for the night," she explained. "I must say everyone at the B and B was full of talk when I mentioned your engagement. They seem very enthusiastic about getting you into the family, Gretch. In fact, no one could talk about anything else. You're creating quite a stir."

Gretchen's heart plummeted through her body, knowing that this was the first anyone at the Big Sky had heard about the engagement. She hazarded a tentative look at David who was grinning broadly. Wicked man. How were they going to explain their way out of this one?

"It's the badge," he conceded solemnly. "And the attitude. My mother is just happy that I'm settling down with a woman who can protect me from potential villains."

For a moment Karen looked startled. Then her eyes twinkled. "Gretchen really is going to have to put a leash on you," she said. "A man who can grin and tease and look like you do is almost too much man to handle. How are you going to deal with him, Gretch?"

Gretchen smiled sweetly. "Handcuffs," she said calmly.

David raised one brow. "For you or for me?"

Karen chuckled. "This is going to be one interesting marriage. I can't wait for the ceremony itself. Have you set the date?"

Gretchen's heart began to hammer. This bet had been

a bad idea altogether. "Not yet," she said, looking to David for backup.

"We don't want to be rushed," he said, his voice low. "Gretchen and I want to have time to go slowly, to let our relationship simmer…and burn…and bubble over until the time is totally, completely right. Until we just can't wait to be together," he said, gazing directly into Gretchen's eyes, his own expression one of unveiled lust.

For a moment Gretchen felt as if everything in the room had dropped away until there was only this man, this feeling, this moment.

"Whoa," Karen said, fanning herself with her hand. "I can see why you were finally forced to give in and change your mind about marrying, Gretchen. I—I suppose I should have called before I just barged in."

Her words seemed to serve as an alarm to David. He took in a breath, allowed the desire to drain from his expression and smiled reassuringly at Karen.

"Forgive me," he said. "I'm afraid I tend to forget myself where Gretchen is concerned. And please, don't apologize for anything. You're not barging in. Anyway, I was just on my way to take Goliath for a walk. Why don't the two of you visit while I do that? I'll see both of you later."

He dropped a light kiss on Gretchen's lips before retrieving Goliath's leash and taking him out the door.

"Gretch, how can you stand letting him go for even a few moments?"

It was difficult, Gretchen admitted, watching him go, but she was just going to have to get used to it. In just a few days she was going to have to let him go forever.

* * *

"I can't believe the entire town thinks that we're engaged now," Gretchen whispered, her voice worried as she and David left their cars and walked toward the station the next morning.

"Believe it," David said with a slow, lazy smile. "When I went home to change this morning, the entire family was waiting for me, wearing their best smug smiles. My mother has been patting me on the head all morning, as though I'd just told her I'd won the Nobel prize. My sister berated me over the phone before I left for work today for not telling her that I was getting married. Then she told me that she wanted to hug me for choosing you."

"And I finally had to take the phone off the hook last night," Gretchen said in amazement. "I can't believe how many people care whether or not I get married."

"They love you, sweetheart."

She looked up at him and her heart took a long plunge off a high and rocky peak. He was such a caring man. After Karen had gone last night, he'd made long, slow love to her. He'd made very sure that she'd found pleasure in his arms. He'd taken care of Goliath and brought her breakfast in bed before he'd left her this morning. "I grew up in a house where breakfast was very important," he'd told her. "You need this." And he'd sat there and watched her eat every bite. Like a husband—or maybe a fiancé.

"Admit it," he whispered near her ear, after an elderly couple crossed the street to offer their congratulations. "You're having fun and so is everyone else."

She was. There was something about making everyone so happy with a little news, even erroneous news, that made her feel good. For a split second, she wondered whether she could ever get used to this, if she could ever be a happily married woman. But even the thought sent a thread of panic spiraling through her. She smothered her thoughts.

"Maybe we're having fun and maybe everyone else is, but our engagement is a lie," she said.

"But not a mean-spirited one," he maintained. "No one's being hurt. And when I get ready to leave, we'll tell everyone that we've decided to just remain best friends. They'll spend all their time hoping we'll get back together and even that can be fun for some of them. Lily Mae will eat it up. Until then, let's enjoy our freedom."

And he turned her toward him, slid his arm behind her back and lifted her lips to his in a dipping, searing kiss.

Her feet left the ground, she pressed her palms to his chest to balance herself, and then she forgot everything except the heat of David's touch, the soap-and-man scent of him, the pleasure of his mouth against hers.

When he finally pulled back slowly and balanced her on unsteady legs, a round of applause could be heard from across the street.

"David, how are you going to keep your mind on the business of keeping the peace if you're thinking about kissing Gretchen all the time?"

David raised his head and grinned. "Kissing Gretchen clears the fog out of my mind," he said in a low teasing voice.

"Then kiss her again," the man called with a whoop of laughter.

But Gretchen, not to be outdone, wasn't about to let

David call all the shots. She stood on her toes until she was almost eye-to-eye with David, looped her arm around his neck and slanted her lips to his own.

"Now," she said when her head was spinning and she had pulled back from the temptation of David, "I'm more than ready to face a day's work."

"If you should feel the need to do that again anytime today, love, feel free. Go right ahead and press your body against mine," David said as they entered the station. "Could make for an extremely interesting day."

It had been, as David said, an interesting day. Gretchen had talked to Reba at the lab and been told that since they were almost finished with a backlog of work, she could expect the results on her hair and skin samples very soon. She and David had rescued a woman whose car had rolled over and ended up in a ditch. They'd also taken some good-natured ribbing about their engagement, but it had been fun and freeing to be able to show her attraction to him without worrying about what people would think.

Now they were settling down to a relaxed dinner at the Hip Hop before heading for home.

"Nice ring, Gretchen," Emma said as she came over to the table with her coffeepot. "When are you going to get married?"

David looked at Gretchen's flustered expression. He felt a little bad for having dragged her into this situation, but not too bad.

"We thought…next spring," he said suddenly, delighting in Gretchen's wide-eyed shocked gaze. "I always liked June."

She turned those delicious green eyes on him. "Why

wait until June?" she asked in a low, sultry tone. "When May is so much…fresher."

The sound of chairs shifting sounded throughout the diner. David risked a glance away from Gretchen and noticed that they'd snagged the attention of almost everyone in the place. He could tell from the way Gretchen's eyes shifted slightly that she'd noticed the same thing. Dinner had never been conducted so silently at the Hip Hop, he'd just bet.

"May is good," he agreed with a lazy smile. "Even better than June, really."

"Oh, Gretch, look how he went along with you on that. Isn't that sweet? I love a romantic man," one woman in the fourth booth proclaimed. "You'll have the wedding here in Whitehorn, won't you?"

David raised one brow.

"I wouldn't have it any other way," Gretchen agreed, lowering her lashes to hide the amusement he knew he'd find there if he only looked in her eyes. "Karen and Pamela will come and all my family. And the bridesmaids will all wear sea-green. It's my favorite color."

David grinned at the game she'd entered into so gamely.

"It suits you," he assured her. "Turns your eyes that misty green I can't resist. Those eyes of yours make me feel sort of wild and untamed, Gretchen."

David leaned closer, gazing into those bewitching eyes, and Gretchen parted her lips just a breath. The tea-kettle clock on the wall ticked loudly in the ensuing fascinated silence. A robber could have come in and walked off with everyone's dinner right then and no one would have stopped him. Or even noticed that he was there, so intent was every diner on the scenario at Gretchen and David's table.

David finally keyed in on the silence. He shook his head to clear his mind. "As for the wedding day," he continued with some effort, "I have friends with musical backgrounds. We'll hold the ceremony at the Big Sky with dinner and dancing afterward. We'll open up the gardens, set tables up around the lake if you like."

"I like," she answered softly. "And I'll like it even better if you wear a black tux. You look sinfully handsome in black and white," Gretchen told him in a low, provocative voice.

"Wear something sexy," David whispered, reaching across the table to cup his hand around her neck and pull her closer to him. "I don't care if it's white. Just sexy."

Someone dropped a glass. It shattered, and Gretchen jerked upright.

David drank in a long gulp of air. He shook his head and grinned at the other customers, tossing money down onto the table to pay for their meal.

"Well, this has been enjoyable. Great seeing everyone," he said cheerily as he rose and reached for Gretchen's hand. "But now it's time to get the lady back home to her bed. Good night."

She blushed, and it was a precious sight even though he knew the heat in her cheeks would embarrass her. Gretchen prided herself on being strong and tough.

"Good night," she said to Emma and to those who were calling their farewells. David held open the door and she stepped outside.

The door had barely floated shut behind them when she looked up at him, both brows raised.

"Well," she said, "that was certainly entertaining for everyone, wasn't it?"

David laughed and then he indulged himself by doing exactly what he wanted to do and what everyone else wanted him to do, too. He picked Gretchen up, swung her around and kissed her.

Her mouth was cool and sweet. She kissed him back.

"It was certainly entertaining for me," he agreed.

"But now it *is* time to go home," she whispered, her breath feathering over his lips in a honeyed caress. "The day is over."

"And the night is beginning."

She didn't answer, and that in itself was the answer. The one he wanted. All in all, it had been a wonderful day, and there was only more to come.

Gretchen listened to the comfortable sound of her steps and David's clicking together against the sidewalk. It was late as they made their way back to the station so that she could pick up some paperwork she'd left there. It was later still as they stepped back through the doorway onto the sidewalk. They'd spent much of their day piecing together the testimonies of all the people they'd interviewed about Raven, rearranging the information, jotting down scenarios they might have missed. Something just didn't quite fit and she meant to find what it was. But for now, they'd put that behind them for the day. David was heading for his car and she was heading to hers. As if they were going to their separate homes. And they were. But in a little more than an hour he'd be with her again. He'd claim that he'd come to walk Goliath, and he would do that, but then he'd also come to her bed.

Gretchen shivered at the thought, vaguely uneasy at

how deeply David always seemed to affect her. She'd enjoyed that scene at the Hip Hop way too much. It had been fun and fast and wild and so very David. She hoped that she'd get over him easily when he left.

I will, she promised herself. She'd always done whatever she'd had to do. This time would be no different.

"Goodbye, Gretchen," he said, drawing out her name in that slightly sensual way he had as he kissed her once, hard, and moved away, stepping off the sidewalk.

"Goodbye," she said softly, barely resisting the urge to touch her lips.

He had turned away, she was pulling her keys from her pocket, ready to step off the sidewalk just as he had, when he turned to smile at her once more.

A scraping sound came from above and David looked up. Instead of the smile she saw his eyes turn dark and dangerous.

"Gretchen, move!" he yelled, and then before she could act, he launched himself at her, snagged her around the waist and rolled with her to the ground, cushioning her fall with his body. As her teeth clamped together in a sharp clack inside her head, she heard a loud crack.

She looked to where she had been standing and saw a large rock smashed in two on the concrete.

"Go back inside," David whispered, whisking her off him as he leaped to his feet and raced for the back of the building where the fire escape was located.

She struggled to stand and ran for the fire escape herself, keeping David in her sights.

David threw himself up the metal stairs and scrambled to the top, not worrying about the noise he was making. At other times he could run as silently as a cat, but here he had a need for speed and no time to worry about being careful.

Someone had tried to hurt Gretchen, damn it, and that someone was going to pay.

He cleared the fire escape, swinging onto the tar-papered roof. In the distance, he could see someone—a small adult or a kid—scurrying over the rooftops. David threw on some speed, leaped the few feet from one roof to the other and cut the distance in two.

The noise of his footsteps getting closer had the man turning to look over his shoulder, stumbling, scrambling to get back up, and taking off again, swinging over the side of a roof.

In the short time he had, David skidded on the tar paper, made it to the spot where the guy had disappeared and vaulted over the side himself. Sliding down one railing and then the next, he made it to the first floor platform, jumped over the side and dropped lightly to the ground. The mop-topped, black-haired man jumped on him. David tossed him over his shoulder but the wild-eyed heavily muscled attacker landed on his feet. Butting David with his head, he knocked him off-balance, pulled out a knife, and slid the blade into his hand, aiming to throw it. David feinted, and the knife missed, but his move was enough to give the man some time. Snatching up the knife and sliding into the street, the thug threw himself into a car and took off.

David could only watch the car skid away.

A clicking behind him caught his attention and he turned to see Gretchen clearing the last steps of the fire escape.

He frowned and she put her hands on her hips.

"Don't even mention the fact that I didn't hide in the station, David, if you know what's good for you. You know I couldn't do that."

He dragged in air, and nodded curtly. "Did you recognize him?"

She shook her head. "Never saw him, and that car he took belongs to Joe, one of the ushers at the movie theater. I try to tell people to lock their cars, but this is Whitehorn."

"Might as well tell them to fly without wings," he agreed. "Come on, let's go see if we can get a composite photo out and start a hunt for this guy."

"I was just going to say that," she said.

"I know you were," he said in a gruff whisper, suddenly dragging her against him and holding her to his heart. "I know just what you were going to say. Gretchen, I know something else, too. You're not going to like it."

She looked up at him, her eyes wide. "If you're going to point out that I'm trembling, then don't. I wasn't scared for myself. I never saw the rock until it hit the ground. I was halfway down the stairs when he went for you. That knife he tossed your way could have ended it for you, David."

"It didn't," was all he said. "And that wasn't what I was going to say."

"Tell me, then," she whispered, moving closer against him.

"I just wanted you to know that I intend to stick close to you for the next few days. Don't argue with me."

She didn't answer, but her lips were cool and giving when he pulled her against him. She knew that he needed to be macho about this, and for his sake, she was going to let him, it seemed. For a few days, at least.

Thank goodness for a woman who knew when to talk and when to kiss. For a few days, at least, he could still have her for his own.

And heaven help any man who tried to take her from him.

Thirteen

With not much to go on, they hadn't identified her assailant. But that wasn't exactly surprising, Gretchen thought two days later. The fact that he had tried to attack her didn't necessarily mean that he was someone she would know or remember. The fact was that she wore a badge. She'd been in law enforcement for years, and that meant making enemies at times. She'd made more than her share in Miami and a few in Elk Springs and even Whitehorn, as well. He could be someone she'd once put in jail, someone who knew someone she'd put in jail, or he could be a man who just didn't like cops, or women, or blondes, for that matter. The newspapers were filled with people who hated for a living, and trying to make rhyme or reason out of such things could make a person crazy.

That didn't mean they hadn't tried to connect the man in some way to the work she was doing at the moment, but the truth was that thinking that way could lead a person down a lot of wrong alleys. She and David now had another investigation on their hands, they'd sent out a drawing of the man and as much information as they had. They'd asked for witnesses or information, but so far they had nothing. And while she was being careful, Gretchen wasn't losing sleep over this incident.

"I couldn't live that way," she told David. "Neither could you. Looking over your shoulder is part of what we do, but looking over your shoulder all the time and never looking forward means you've become ineffective at your work."

"Sweet lady, I love it when you're logical," he said, dropping a kiss on her bare breast and then moving his mouth up to cover her lips.

She chuckled against his lips. "You know darn well I haven't needed to look over my shoulder anyway. You've been watching me like an overprotective bear."

"You don't like the way I've been treating you?" he asked, sweeping his hand down between their bodies and driving all thought from her mind for several seconds.

When she was able to control herself at all, she took long deep breaths, shuddering at his touch.

"I love the way you treat me," she confessed. And barely brushing his skin, she slowly walked her fingers down his chest and lower. Lower still. She gently closed her fingertips around the tip of his shaft.

He stopped breathing, she was sure of it, though his heart slammed against his chest and echoed into her own. He endured the exquisite torture of her barely there touch until he was shuddering deep inside. Then he lifted her leg, parted her and drove deep into her depths. He shattered her, destroyed her, and had her asking for more.

When they finally came up for breath, he smoothed the hair back from her forehead and kissed the damp skin there. "I love the way you treat me," he said, repeating her words. "And I thank you for letting me fuss. I have nightmares about that moment when that rock nearly fell on you. I'm not going to let anything happen to you as long as I can prevent it. And when I go—"

"When you go, I'll be fine." She grabbed the hand he was caressing her with, took it between both of her palms and kissed it. "I'm a big girl, David, and anyway, everyone in the department is looking out for everyone else since that incident. No one's taking any chances. I won't take any chances," she promised.

"Then we'll be okay," he finally said as he eased into her again.

"We'll be wonderful," she whispered as they traveled to a world scattered with bright stars. She smiled against his skin and he smiled against hers and they waited for the morning together.

Lyle Brooks crushed a cigarette under his shoe as if it gave him great pleasure to extinguish the life of something.

He bit off a harsh expletive.

The Cheyenne were still not cooperating. He'd given them his best smooth talk, his clearest arguments. They didn't want his arguments. They wanted what they'd agreed to in the first place. They pointed out that they were old hands at the bait-and-switch game. He had to give them credit. They were no fools, even if he did hate every last sorry one of them.

And as for the real fools—or rather, fool, there was

no question who that was. The idiot had made a mess of things. He'd been told to make things look like an accident. Who would believe that a rock falling from the sky was an accident?

"Nobody," he whispered, his voice a thin rasp of sound squeezed from a mouth thinned by rage.

Now he'd have to handle things himself. He'd already taken care of the fool. Only one more to go. Or maybe two.

He had to get the man out of the way and that wouldn't be easy. It hadn't been easy. David Hannon was like water running along the ground, impossible to separate from the sand it flowed into. He took his watchdog duties with Gretchen Neal very seriously. Still, sooner or later the guy had to let down his guard. They always let down their guard, didn't they?

Then, he thought calmly, then he would finish his business with the woman. Eventually he'd convince the leaders of the Laughing Horse Reservation to make the trade of the land.

And the sapphires would be his and only his. He would finally have the last word and the last laugh and the money.

He was going to be the greatest Kincaid ever known.

David rubbed the frown from between his brows and tried not to think of Gretchen. The woman had been too much a part of his thoughts from the very start, but now since that time three days ago when he'd seen that rock hurtling down toward her, he'd been unable to dislodge her from his mind for even the shortest period of time. He was, quite simply, besotted with her. And he was pretty darn sure he was in love with her. It was a damned shame, because she'd made it clearer than clear that she only wanted a short, mad fling.

Oh, they were having that, all right. Every time he plunged into her body, he went mad for her. He wasn't so humble that he didn't know that she reacted the same way to him, but that was all it was for her. She was happy with this. True, she might miss him for a few days when he was gone, but she was the type of woman who would prefer missing him over complicating her life with visions of things that would only be a prison for her. And he couldn't, he absolutely couldn't, try to force his feelings on her. If he ever damaged her spirit, her heart, or her pride, there'd be no way around the fact that he deserved a strong, solid kick in the pants. It just wasn't going to happen.

And so, he'd been hovering. Caring. Wanting. He'd been going damned near insane. It had to stop. Now.

The phone rang beside him.

"Hannon," he said, practically barking into the receiver.

"Whoa, buddy. What have you been eating for breakfast that's turned you into a ticked-off grizzly?" Sascha's voice was laced with humor, but also a familiar trace of concern.

"Rocks," David said, knowing someday he'd tell his friend just how close that answer was to the truth. But not today. He couldn't talk about Gretchen today. And maybe not anytime in the near future.

"What can I do for you, Sasch?" he asked. "You need an ear to listen? Bridget still on your mind?"

"Bridget's yesterday," his friend said. "And you know me, David. I'm on to someone else. A luscious redhead named Terri. You know the rules of the game. Win some, lose some. Always move on. Always enjoy."

David knew the rules of the game or what they were supposed to be. They just didn't apply where Gretchen was concerned. She was special, different. She'd taken the rule book and ripped out the pages.

"What can I do for you, Sasch?" he asked again.

"Not for me. For Phil," Sascha said. "He's in D.C., but I got a call from him. There's new info on the Tedrin case that might finally make a difference and break things open for someone who knows the particulars. That would be you, bud, as well you know. Time to give up this life with the locals and get back to the federal world. Phil asked me to fax the papers to you in the Billings office so you could make a determination of what the next step should be. It's confidential stuff, of course. You'll be all right picking it up there?"

"Sure." Of course he'd be all right. His work had always had his heart, and this was probably just what he needed to get his life back where it belonged. Action. Results. Something to occupy his thoughts and his time. "You fax it. I'll deal with it," he promised. "Thanks for the message, Sasch. I needed this."

"David? You okay?"

"Yeah. I'm okay. Just needed something to do with my time, I guess," he said. "You know how it is when you're sitting on your hands."

"Don't I? Yeah." He paused a moment, then, "You're not getting in over your head in the heart department, are you? Not losing it over that lady cop of yours? Not doing anything stupid?"

David hesitated for half a second. Of course he was doing something stupid. He'd been making mistakes with Gretchen from day one. It was time to stop.

"David?"

"Not doing anything stupid, Sasch," David managed to say smoothly. "Do I ever?"

Sascha's chuckle was low. "You're right. What was I thinking of? This is David I'm talking about. The guy who never commits. All right, buddy. I'm glad things are good with you. See you in a few days. Take care."

And the line went dead.

David waited for Gretchen to emerge from Rafe's office. When she did, he gave her a smile. "You'll be happy to know that your shadow has to leave for a short while. Business in Billings."

"Your business or mine?"

He grinned. "You think I'd keep you in the dark about your own work?"

She studied him for a minute, then shook her head. "No. You're a bit overprotective," she said, smoothing his collar and then kissing him, "but you're fair. You want to swing by the house when you're done?"

"Ah, I see," he said, teasing her with his lips. "You're just afraid I won't be back in time to walk Goliath. You only want me for my skill with animals."

She smiled against his lips. "I adore your skill with animals, and your skill with...other things. Maybe there's a little animal in you. Maybe Goliath recognizes a kindred spirit—or at least a kindred male."

"He still mooning over that little Pomeranian?"

Gretchen nodded and the lemony scent of her went through him. Her hair brushed against his skin and his senses. "She's a tease, I think. He's frantic to have her."

"I'm frantic to have you, too," he whispered, pulling her closer, pulling her around the corner of the file cabinet so no one could hear and no one could see.

"Then come by my house when you're done. Will it be long?"

He shook his head. "I can be there and back in just a few hours."

"I'll meet you at home when I get off work," she promised.

"If you leave here for any reason other than to go home, you take a partner," he warned.

She frowned. "David, I know the rules. If it's something that warrants extra muscle or extra care, I take a partner. I'll be careful," she promised.

He caught her to him for one last kiss before he marched out the door on the way back to his future.

The information from the lab came in just as Gretchen was getting ready to go out the door for the day.

And there were no real surprises, but there was, at last, hard evidence. She still didn't know why she'd been hearing rumors that Lyle Brooks had been hounding the Cheyenne to make a land switch that just didn't make sense. But she knew enough to take the next step. Some of the puzzle pieces had finally stopped spinning around and locked into place.

Now she had proof. A man's life had been taken. It had been stolen, not by an accident but by an intentional act. And so she finally had room to move, to act, to do what she had been trained to do, Gretchen thought.

She sat for a few seconds concentrating on the information she'd been given, realizing that at last one criminal at least would be taken off the streets.

It wouldn't bring back the life of an innocent man or help his family deal with their pain and grief. Those kinds of miracles didn't happen, but she could at least make sure that no one else suffered at the hands of that scumbag. As always, it had to be enough. It was the nature of the job.

"So let's take care of business," she whispered as she picked up the phone. Punching in the number of the cellular in David's car, she listened through the rings and hoped he had taken care of his own business. If she had to, she would take another officer, but after all his time and effort, David deserved to be the one to partner her on this arrest.

The ringing came to an abrupt halt.

"Hannon." David's deep strong voice washed over her, even distance and the slight haziness of the connection not dulling the reaction she had yet to get accustomed to.

"David, it's Gretchen. I just got word from Reba. Hair and skin were found under Peter Cook's fingernails that matched the samples I took from Lyle. How far away are you?"

"Fifteen minutes tops," he said.

"Good. I'll meet you at the house and save you the trouble of driving all the way into the center of town and back out again. We'll hook up and make the arrest from there."

"On my way," he confirmed as she said goodbye and hung up the phone.

There was a sense of rightness in going to meet David, Gretchen thought as she climbed into her car and started the ignition, and a sense of relief. And it went beyond what she felt in his arms or how she felt about him as a man. She'd learned to trust him in these past few weeks. He'd learned to trust her. In spite of all her initial reservations about the man, his family, and the unusual nature of his request to be in on her cases, they'd worked well together. Arresting Lyle would be like adding sprinkles to the ice cream. A sweet bonus.

She drove the short distance to her house. No sign of David yet, but then, she hadn't expected it.

Turning her key and clicking open the door to the cottage, she waited for Goliath to greet her with his usual patter and gleeful bark. The patter never materialized. The bark was loud and clear and distressed. She noticed for the first time that the bedroom door was closed.

"Goliath?"

Her answer was a frustrated and frantic whining.

She moved to the door, pushed it back.

The wildly rolling eyes of her dog met her own gaze as Goliath barked and scuffled over the floor, jumping up on her, clearly anxious.

"What's wrong, boy? I didn't lock you in there somehow this morning, did I? I'm sorry. No wonder you're so upset."

Gretchen knelt to soothe her hand over Goliath's head, but his barking didn't stop. He flung his head around, looking behind him.

She turned to see what he was looking at and an arm hauled her up, a gloved hand clamping over her mouth. The taste of old leather and the scent of sweat and heavy cologne assaulted her. She was dragged backward against an unyielding body.

Her fingers automatically went for her gun. Too late. They slid away as the gun was dragged from its holster and tossed aside.

The cold and oily smell of steel drifted to her as the hard snub of her assailant's revolver was shoved right under her chin.

"Don't worry about your little dog, Neal," a low, unpleasant and all too familiar voice told her. "He's just a tad upset that you weren't here to greet a visitor. He had to handle all the duties of hosting by himself. Can you blame him?"

Sheer panic rose up in her and she fought to calm herself.

Think, Gretchen, think! Don't fight. He'll be expecting that. He'll be prepared for that, so don't fight. At least not yet.

Yet as Goliath lunged at Lyle, the urge to fight was there. Goliath was trying to nip at Lyle and she wanted to do the same.

"Call him off," Lyle said, kicking out at the little dog as Goliath took a nip again.

She held her tongue.

Lyle shoved the hard butt of the gun harder against her throat. He pulled back his foot to kick just as Goliath recovered from the roll he'd taken and headed in to try again.

"Goliath, sit," she ordered.

The little dog ignored her. She remembered what she'd told David about him, how he'd been considered untrainable. But he'd always obeyed her since she'd worked with him. Until now.

The gun bit into her flesh harder. Gretchen nearly choked as the press of steel nudged at her windpipe.

She swallowed hard, opening her mouth. The pressure of the gun let up just a touch.

"Sit, Goliath," she said again, aiming for a calm tone, fearful for both the little dog's life as well as her own. Reluctantly, Goliath did as he was told. His little body wiggled, he whimpered, but he obeyed.

And now the reality of the situation shoved in on her. David wasn't that far away. He was barreling toward her. And he didn't know there was an ambush waiting behind her door.

She had to disarm Lyle, trip him up somehow. But how?

"Why did you come here?" she managed to say in spite of the press of metal to flesh. "What is it you want?"

An eerie chuckle rolled through Lyle's wiry body and the sound echoed through the arm he was crushing against her.

"Oh, I think you know," he said. "You see, I'm a businessman and I don't exactly like anyone interfering in my business interests. I especially don't like it when someone keeps pushing me, when someone all but accuses me of something. And I really don't like it when anybody repeatedly comes between me and what I want. Now, Ms. Neal, you've closed down the excavation of my resort, you've insinuated that I might have something to do with the death of one of my employees. How do you think all of this is going to affect future business developments? People don't want to conduct transactions with a man who can't control his business."

"And what would that business be, Lyle?" She spat out the words. "What did Peter Cook do that caused you to kill him?"

The arm that was holding her jerked and tightened. Gretchen struggled for breath. She worked to maintain her control. She did her best to not think of David. If she did, she would panic. She would lose.

"You killed him, didn't you?" she said, her voice as cool as she could make it.

His chilling laughter sent shivers slipping down her spine.

"Neal, haven't I told you it was an accident? And yet, you've never believed me. Not like everyone else. I have to say I admire you for sticking it out and not following the crowd. It's amazing what people will believe if you set the scene just right."

"Why?" She forced herself to not react or move, forced her mind to think about what she could do to warn David rather than what this dirtbag was saying. Maybe if she could keep him talking, she would have time to plan, to ready herself.

"Why?" he echoed. "You mean, why did I kill Cook? He did something stupid. Just like you, Neal. If you hadn't pushed me, you'd be just fine. Now you're dead. Let's go." He pulled the gun from her throat and shoved it into her back.

She considered not moving for just a second, but if she couldn't outwit Brooks and he killed her here, David would come in and find them—and then he'd be dead, too.

Fear and pain and distress reared up in her. She fought to shove them aside.

She had to stay alert and alive, to give herself time to think. Time was what she needed the most. Time and luck. But she would have neither if she broke down. And she would have nothing if David died, if she let him walk in on this, if she didn't move now.

Gretchen moved.

Lyle slithered in closer behind her, like a guard—or a lover. One arm was looped over her shoulder in what might be presumed to be a friendly embrace. His jacket hung open slightly, enclosing her. His gun was concealed between his body and hers.

"This is cozy, isn't it, Detective?" he asked in a harsh, laughing whisper. "Your car, please. I'm afraid mine isn't here. I guess I left it in my driveway where everyone could see it."

That laugh again. Gretchen wondered if anyone had ever actually smiled at this man's laughter.

"Sorry, you'll have to drive," he said as he edged her in the passenger door and followed her inside. "I seem to need my hands," he said, wiggling the gun just a bit.

She slid over the gearshift to the driver's seat, the gun following her, low on the seat, pointing up at her.

"Don't move more than you need to in order to drive the car. Don't make any wrong turns. Don't act like a dumb cop, Neal," Lyle said quietly as he gestured for her to start the car. "If you follow directions, your boyfriend might survive. I understand he's leaving town soon. He's not a danger to me. So just be a good girl and follow the rules. I know you know how to do that. Isn't that what they teach you about in cop school?

He laughed again as if he'd said something funny and Gretchen pulled out onto the street. She could, as he said, swerve the car, but she'd be dead long before the car crashed—and Lyle might survive.

"Where are we going?" she asked.

"Nowhere anyone will find you real soon, Neal. You'll simply disappear. No body to trace. We'll find a good place to stash you. Make no mistake about that."

"How did you know I was on my way to arrest you?"

A long silence filled the car. When Gretchen turned to look at Lyle, he was grinning, his eyes narrowed in glee.

"You were coming to arrest me? Now that makes this so much better. Not that I didn't think you'd do just that in time, but actually I had no idea. I've been following you for days now. Only problem is you never seem to be alone. Today I saw your guard dog ride out and I took my opportunity the way I always do. It's one of my most endearing qualities, I'm sure. But as for your coming to arrest me, well, Neal, I'm flattered that you would come alone. Maybe you really do care."

And maybe she'd better shut her mouth, Gretchen thought, before Lyle figured out that someone else would be looking for him really soon.

Lyle wouldn't be happy to see another cop. He'd be angry, desperate, and desperate men tended to shoot wildly and repeatedly.

A trickle of fear found its way in. It drizzled right through her. This morning the world had seemed bright. Now her life was at stake. And the life of the man she loved hung in the balance, as well.

Gretchen didn't take the time to refute the fact that she loved David or that the thought of anything happening to him filled her with anguish right now. When a madman was holding a gun against you, there was no point in lying to yourself.

The fact was that she loved David desperately.

The fact was that if she didn't survive, she'd never see him again.

Gretchen drove, mindful of the turns she was making, up the mountain pathways that normally looked so beautiful, around steep turns heavily packaged in lodgepole pines that hid the curling road behind her from view.

In a matter of minutes they had left civilization and all hope of rescue behind.

She was on her own. Just her, her training, and a man who had nothing to lose by killing her.

Fourteen

David rounded the last turn leading to Gretchen's house. He was still two blocks away, but on the deserted street he was close enough to see her car pull out of the driveway.

His first thought was that she had tired of waiting for him and was moving off to arrest Lyle Brooks alone.

"No," he decided. She was brave but also bright and she was honorable. She'd said she'd meet him here. If she was leaving, there was a reason. A good reason. Something important enough to have her leaving when she knew he'd be arriving any moment.

David maintained a distance, but he slid right past her drive, moving off in the direction she had gone.

He leaned forward, straining to see her. Two heads visible. Could be anyone. A tall woman, a small man. Her friend Karen, his sister, or someone else, he thought as she took a turn leading out of town.

Something didn't feel right here.

An emergency call? Maybe, but then she would have radioed for assistance. Maybe she had. If so, there was no problem. He'd find out when they got there.

And if the other person in the car was a man?

"Then she'll know you for the jealous fool you are when this is over, Hannon," he muttered. And there would be hell to pay all around.

But this soul-deep fear that was growing within him with every passing curve of the road didn't feel like jealousy, and anyway, Gretchen had been very open about her involvement with him. There was no one else for her at this point in time. He knew that. He was just reaching for logical solutions, grasping, hoping that there was some ordinary reason Gretchen was headed out of town without him in the opposite direction from the one they would have taken to go to arrest Lyle Brooks.

And as she turned onto a dirt road that led to nowhere, stark fear rushed through David. Gretchen was in that car. There was someone with her, and he was almost dead sure he knew who it was.

The urge to speed up was so great, he could feel his foot pressing the accelerator closer to the floor without any conscious intention of doing so.

He muttered a foul curse and forced himself to ease up a bit. In spite of the twists and turns of this road, he couldn't risk following too closely. If he drove up to Gretchen while Brooks had her in his grasp, it was anyone's guess what the man would do. Whatever the answer was, it wouldn't be good.

"If anything happens to her, Hannon…" He couldn't finish the sentence. Letting his mind go down that road was unacceptable. He'd flay the man alive and feed his body to the nearest bear if he so much as broke one of Gretchen's fingernails.

That was his last thought before he rounded a turn and saw a quick flash of white and chrome. Gretchen's car pulling into a deeply forested part of the woods.

"Nowhere to go here," he muttered. Once the car was in the trees, it would be hidden from view of the road, which was most likely all that Brooks was looking for. A good hiding place for a body.

David sucked in a breath. He rolled his own car to a stop and got out, leaving the door ajar as he slipped onto the grass and began to follow.

"Stop here. Get out slowly." Lyle fired commands like bullets from a semiautomatic.

Gretchen edged her way out of the car. All the way here she'd done her best to talk Lyle into letting her go without revealing that she had hard evidence against him. If he knew that, then he'd realize that David wasn't just going to go away. He'd consider him a threat, as well—and he'd go after him.

Now she was running out of things to say to Lyle and running out of time. A thread of terror slipped in.

"No time for that."

"What?" Brooks practically shouted the word and Gretchen realized that she'd actually spoken out loud, her nervousness getting the best of her.

In spite of her complete aversion to the man, she stayed as close to him as he would allow. If she got the chance, now that her hands were free of the steering wheel, she'd go for the gun or whatever else she could grab to throw him off balance.

Nothing, she thought, her eyes quickly taking in her

surroundings, the small clearing up ahead where he was leading her. He'd chosen well. There was nothing in this clearing for her to latch on to, nowhere to hide for the first twenty or thirty feet if she ran, but there was plenty of cover to hide a body once the deed was done. Acres and acres of trees well away from any inhabited territory. He'd been right when he said that no one would ever find her here.

But he was wrong if he thought that no one would at least look. Reba knew about the matching hair and skin samples. And David knew. He'd look. If there was any way of finding her, any evidence at all of where she'd been taken, he'd dig it out. But not in time. Not nearly in time. And maybe he'd lose his life, too. She fought the pain, but couldn't keep from closing her eyes for a second in a last failed attempt to blot it out.

"Over here," Lyle ordered, wrestling her to a large flat rock. "Kneel. I have a tremendous urge to see you at my feet begging."

She wondered if she would do that when it came to the end. She hoped not, especially since there was no way it would do any good. This was a man without feeling, without a conscience.

Gretchen couldn't help but move when he shoved, but she did her best to keep her feet. If he was going to kill her, if there was no way she could make an escape, she wouldn't give him the pleasure of letting him shoot her execution style, or of watching her run so that he could put a bullet in her back.

I'm sorry, David, she thought. Sorry for what, she didn't know. She'd been going to meet him. She hadn't planned on going it alone this time. But this would hurt him. She knew that, and she wished she could change that.

Brooks narrowed his eyes at her stubborn struggle to stay upright. He caressed his gun against her cheek and started to pull it back into position for firing.

A slight movement against brush sounded in the trees. Like a squirrel or a chipmunk tripping over a twig. Gretchen moved just a touch.

Lyle laughed and grabbed her, holding the gun to her temple.

"I don't think our furry friend is going to save you, beautiful," he whispered.

"Move your finger one hundredth of a centimeter on that trigger and I'll donate your internal organs to the vultures, Brooks."

David's voice was like the inside of a butcher's freezer, icy, crisp and deadly to those who didn't recognize the danger.

Gretchen felt the tremor—of fear or anger—go through Lyle as he swung her around to face his attacker, never letting the gun drop from its deadly position, planting her body firmly between himself and David.

"Well, well, look here, Neal, your boyfriend's come calling, after all. What could be more perfect? Here I thought I wouldn't have to bother with him, but now this works out so much better. With everyone well aware that the two of you are engaged, I won't have to plant much information at all to make them think you've eloped and left town together."

"You won't have to do anything at all, Brooks. You'll be dead."

The gun jostled against Gretchen's temple as Lyle shook his head.

"Sorry, you'll be the one dead, Hannon."

Gretchen didn't need to see the man's face to know that he was smiling, and she knew then that in spite of the gun, it wasn't her life that was in the most immediate danger right now. It was David's. If Brooks shot her, David would kill him before he'd finished squeezing the trigger. But with her as a shield, David couldn't shoot to protect himself right now. Time enough to kill her after David was gone. Time had run out.

Almost.

She had to act now and she knew exactly what she had to do. Looking straight into the eyes of the man she loved, she opened her mouth.

"They'll find you after we're gone, Lyle," she said quietly, never taking her eyes off David, trying her darnedest to send him a message he could read. "I was coming to arrest you, because those hair and skin samples I took from you matched what was found beneath Peter's fingernails. He didn't die from an accidental fall. You pushed him, and it's no secret anymore. Don't think you're safe."

She blinked her eyes and David blinked back. He didn't even nod, but she had to believe that he knew what she intended. She needed to believe that they had, indeed, become partners in the closest sense.

"He fell," Lyle said, his voice agitated. "I just tried to save him. He clutched at me. That's why my skin's underneath his nails."

"That's not what you said," she said, her voice sinking even lower, growing even more accusing. "When your original testimony was taken, you stated that Peter was alive when you left him."

She forced herself not to tense up. She only had time to blink her eyes firmly once more, but as the last word left her mouth, Gretchen dropped bonelessly. She brought her leg up in as smooth an arc as she could manage, aiming for Lyle's chin.

The blow knocked him sideways, but he recovered quickly, swearing as he latched back onto the gun he had nearly dropped. He turned in a wild swoop, firing at David.

But David had dropped low just as Gretchen had moved, as she'd hoped he would. He dodged Brooks's bullet and fired in one rolling movement. One clean shot, but one was all that was necessary. Lyle staggered back and fell.

His gun clattered to the rock. His body relaxed into total stillness.

Gretchen took one look. She didn't need to take a pulse to know that he was dead, but she did it anyway. This man had given Peter Cook no chance. He'd given David and her no chance, but she would give him what little chance she could if it existed. She wouldn't become an animal like him.

But when she touched the skin of the man who would have taken her life without one regret, she found not even the faintest hint of a heart doing its job.

And so she rose—and stepped right into David's arms as he barreled toward her. She looked up into eyes that were still bright and fierce and angry.

"Don't," she said, pushing as close as she could get. "Don't be angry with me right now. You can yell and lecture tomorrow. For today, just kiss me. Hold me."

And he held her as close as two bodies could get without becoming one. He cupped the back of her head in his hand and covered her mouth with his own in a long, desperate, seeking kiss.

"I thought you were gone, Gretchen," he choked. "I thought— I almost wasn't quick enough. I damned near lost you."

"Not yet," she whispered, her voice as desperate as his kiss. His legs gave out and so did hers, and they dropped to the ground beneath them. "Not yet," she repeated, and she twined her arms around his neck. She gave in to the joy creeping up within her. She rained quick, whispery kisses over every inch of David that she could get near.

He ran his palms over every available centimeter of her skin.

Together they reclaimed the day, reclaimed each other. They reclaimed life as they fed each other with kisses and caresses and all the emotion they'd been forced to hold inside during those last few terrible moments.

"How did you know?" she finally asked, pulling back from him long enough to look up into his eyes.

His slow, shaky smile was a relief to see. "I know you," he whispered. "That's what partners do, after all, isn't it? They get to know each other well, well enough to anticipate each other's moves."

He found her lips again, anticipating just what she wanted him to do.

"Come on," he said, pulling her to her feet and into his arms. "Let's get you home. I'll have Rafe send someone back for the body. But for now, you need some time to recover."

She did, and she wanted to do it in David's arms. She wanted to make him forget that he had been forced to kill and she wanted them both to drive away the threat of death that had stared them straight in the face that day.

Then she could face the rest.

She and David weren't over. They were both alive and well and they would survive. But their days as partners were coming to a close.

She would regret that. But for tonight she would have as much of him as she ever could have.

And it would have to be suffice. In two days' time all she would have of David would be achingly sweet and distant memories.

David lay in the dark with Gretchen draped over his chest. He kissed the top of her hair and she snuggled closer in sleep, soothing the rage that still lay banked deep within him.

He'd work through it in time, but it would be a long, slow process to put this day behind him, and he would never, he knew, forget the sight of this lady, a gun pressed to her head, silently telling him that she was about to make a move.

A long, deep river of emotion ran through him. He wondered if he would ever stop loving Gretchen or if he would ever stop wanting to love Gretchen.

He would live without her, because she wanted things that way. He wouldn't intrude on her space because he knew after today that he would do anything, give anything, to see her happy and safe and contented for all eternity.

And contented for Gretchen meant living a single life.

But she couldn't keep him from caring, and neither could he. No matter what he'd done or thought to prevent it, he hadn't been able to back away from what he felt about this slender, strong-willed woman.

She was what made life special. He would have lived in hell forever if she'd died today.

But she'd lived, and it was only right that she be allowed to live on her own terms, in her own way.

He could watch from the sidelines, but he couldn't let himself force his heart on her any more than he could have allowed Lyle Brooks to hurt her and survive.

That was just the way things were.

"So deal with it, buddy," he whispered to himself.

He would. Somehow. But he shook his head as he tried once more to settle down to sleep. How ironic that he'd finally found one woman who could make him want to settle down and make a home, and she happened to be a woman who had absolutely no interest in such things.

Leave it to Gretchen to do things a little differently.

But why not? She was a woman who went along with a ridiculous scheme to pretend she was engaged to him. She was a detective who took the time to listen to people even when she didn't have the time or the ability to solve their problems, just because it made one person's day a little easier to bear. She was a woman who faced the ultimate terror and still managed to keep her thoughts clear enough to stay alive until help could be arranged.

She was, quite simply, he thought, the heart that beat within him.

He shifted and snuggled her just a little closer to him and that small movement jostled her just enough to have her blinking those wide green eyes at him and propping herself up on his chest.

A slow, sweet, sleepy smile lifted her lips. "I'm so glad you're alive, David," she whispered, her voice groggy with sleep. And then she laid her head back on his chest, touched her lips to his skin, making every cell in his body snap to attention as she drifted back into sleep.

As he lay there, smiling into her hair, fighting the instant desire that she had awakened and was now no longer awake to assuage, David felt his heart lurch just slightly.

Tomorrow he was leaving, but there was absolutely no doubt in his mind that Gretchen Neal was going to haunt his sleepless nights for the rest of his life.

And there wasn't a damn thing he could do to fight it.

He settled her closer, kissed her once more and realized that he had no urge to fight anything that had to do with Gretchen.

If he loved her forever—and he would, even if it was to no avail—at least she would be with him in the only way he could have her. In his soul.

Fifteen

She'd been trying her best to keep her mind on work all morning, but Gretchen just couldn't keep her gaze from straying to David again and again. This was his last day. He'd been given his orders and he had to get on a plane back to Atlanta tomorrow. The fact that he'd come in to work at all today amazed her. She knew that yesterday had been hard on both of them, but she suspected that it had been harder on David than herself.

She'd been so busy trying to think her way out of the situation that she hadn't had time to give in to the natural terror that any sane person would feel.

But David—he'd had to watch her life being threatened while his hands were effectively tied. She had a hint of what that must be like, because in those moments when she'd feared David would barge in on her and Lyle and be gunned down, she'd barely beaten back the panic.

And David had been the one who'd had to take a life.

No matter that it hadn't been the life of a good man, and no matter that he'd done it before. He'd confessed that much to her when she'd asked, trying to make sure that he was all right. She'd seen officers who'd been forced to kill before. There was always a bit of fallout. No one came out completely unscathed. And the few who did seem to have no reaction whatsoever were the ones who had to be watched most closely.

David had not been unaffected. She'd seen the acceptance in his eyes and the regret that a life had had to be given for justice to prevail.

But he was here, finishing up the paperwork with her, and mostly—she knew the man too well—offering her his presence. He wanted to make sure that she was past her own reactions to yesterday's bad experience.

Without thought, without the time to prepare herself, her heart overflowed. She had to fight a teary feeling deep inside, and that made her so angry that she slammed the folder she was holding down onto the desk.

David looked up from the scratching of his pen on paper.

"You okay?" he asked.

No, she was not okay. She hadn't been okay since the day she'd met David Hannon.

"I'm perfectly fine," she lied with a smile. Except this man had flipped her world like a top spinning off its string. He had her thinking about her mother and herself and all those years when she'd sworn she'd never follow in her parents' footsteps. He had her wondering if her mother really had regretted all those moves, or if the regrets had only been her own imaginings, her own grumblings. She knew for a fact that her father had regretted having to uproot his family, that her mother had always smiled and reassured him as best she could.

"I wish I could stay and help you work out things on Raven's case," he said, reaching for her hand.

Without thought, she pulled away. Her emotions were much too close to the surface. She had a feeling that tears weren't far behind, and she *never* cried. She made a point of not crying. It was bad for business, especially if you were a female detective. It was unacceptable and left you open to criticism, made people think you couldn't take whatever was dished out. Worst of all, it left you vulnerable. If she let David see she was upset, he would know what she didn't want him to ever know.

She loved him. Completely. Devastatingly. And it just wouldn't do.

Somehow she dredged up a smile. Phony, but it would have to do.

"We'll get through on the case. And I'll be protected," she assured him. "Haven't you noticed all the eyes that have been following my every move today?"

He smiled slightly. "Everyone feels guilty that you were abducted yesterday while the world and the Whitehorn force went on."

She shrugged. "How could they know?"

He frowned. "Exactly."

She leveled a stare at him. "It won't happen again. Rafe's set shadows on me. And, anyway, the danger is past."

"Yes," he said solemnly. But she still heard the doubt in his voice. Both of them knew that in their line of work the danger was never past.

She felt the catch in her throat. David was going

away. He would no doubt put his life on the line over and over and she would never know. She knew now why her mother had calmly packed up her household time and time again. It had been important to her to be with the man she loved beyond life, to see him every day, to know that he was alive and with her, day and night. Her father had, she realized, been her mother's world. Their life had been complicated by her father's work and responsibilities and their constant moves from one place to another, but they'd loved, and they'd raised a houseful of children whom they'd taught how to love.

She didn't regret her childhood, just as David didn't regret what he'd gone through as a child. Her struggles had made her stronger. They'd made her who she was, just as his challenges had made him what he was.

The man she loved. The man who was leaving just when she'd realized she wanted him to stay with her forever. The man she couldn't reach out and latch onto because she knew he had a path of his own to follow. And because he hadn't asked her to share his life. He wouldn't. David Hannon loved women, but he didn't stay with just one.

"Atlanta must be pretty at this time of year," she couldn't help saying, although she wished she could shove the words back into her mouth.

He gave her a deep, lazy smile. He rose and dropped a kiss on her lips. "I'll show you sometime," he whispered.

But he wouldn't, she knew. Because she didn't think she could bear to visit him and go through a goodbye all over again.

"Hey, Hannon," a voice called at that moment, and Gretchen turned to look toward the door. "Your aunt's here to see you."

"Come on," David said, giving her hand a tug. "Come with me. Aunt Celeste came in, I'm sure, to see you alive and in person. Ten to one she brought you comfort food. She needs to know you're all right. And who can blame her?"

"I'm going to get spoiled by all this attention," Gretchen said softly and with a laugh. "Detectives are supposed to face danger, David. They're not supposed to be fussed over."

He stopped midstride and looked over his shoulder. "Baloney, Gretchen. You don't have anything to prove. People love you. Let them fuss. And let yourself enjoy."

She placed her hand on his sleeve. "I do," she assured him. "I will."

The words that were so close to the kinds of vows lovers made as they joined their hands in marriage fell from her lips too easily. She removed her fingers from his arm, wishing she could hold his warmth next to her forever. And she turned to Celeste who wrapped her in a warm hug.

"You should be in bed, sweetie," the older woman ordered. "But David told me I might as well suggest you hang from the ceiling naked, so I brought you brownies instead. Caramel and fudge."

Gretchen grinned at Celeste and hugged her again. "If I were in bed, I'd miss all your good cooking, Celeste. Pretty clever of me to come in and claim all this attention, wasn't it?" she asked with a grin as she bit into a heavenly brownie oozing with melted fudge.

Celeste laughed out loud. She turned to her nephew and opened her mouth to make a comment.

Her mouth opened wider. Her eyes widened like a

gaping door. She brought both hands up to cover her mouth.

"Oh, no," she whispered through the tunnel of her fingers.

Gretchen spun around to see what had distressed Celeste so. Her gaze swept across Storm Hunter who was on the other side of the room deep in conversation with Rafe. Storm's eyes were dark and tired and leveled on David, Celeste and herself. He looked slightly stooped and bleary, as if weariness had left him sleepless of late. But as Gretchen made eye contact with the man, she saw his attention sharpen, she saw him blink. She felt a swoosh of movement at her side.

And she turned to see David catching his aunt in his arms as Celeste slumped toward the floor.

The day had slipped away, David thought as he walked Gretchen to her car that evening. Celeste had been taken home, apologizing to everyone for behaving so foolishly in fainting, in not realizing how closely Storm resembled his brother, Raven. She apologized for thinking even for a second that she'd seen a ghost.

The excitement was over.

And the torture was about to begin.

His bags were packed. He had to say goodbye to Gretchen. How was he ever going to do it and survive? He wanted to kiss her, needed to kiss her, but if he did that now, he was afraid he wouldn't be able to let go.

She solved the problem by holding out her hand.

"Well," she said, her voice the barest trace of shaky sound, "I guess this is where we say goodbye. I wanted—"

She took a deep breath. She bit down on her lip.

He swayed toward her.

"I wanted to thank you," she said, forestalling his movement. "For being such a good partner. A detective couldn't ask for better backup. A woman couldn't ask for a better fiancé."

Her voice shook on those last words. Her fingers were ice-cold when he took them in his own.

And David knew in that moment that he had to warm her. He had to take the risk, he had to do what he'd promised himself he wouldn't do for her sake.

He lifted her hand to his lips, turned it over and kissed the palm deeply, savoring the way her skin warmed beneath his.

"I wanted to make it that easy for you, sweetheart, but I'm afraid it isn't going to be that simple."

She looked up at him. She opened her eyes wide, shaking her head in a mute question. But she didn't retrieve her hand, he noted. She didn't step back from him.

"I don't understand," she finally said.

"You want me to just walk away, but when have I ever just walked away when you wanted me to, Gretchen?"

And her fingers curled closed slightly. She raised her hand as if to touch his cheek, then held her hand there in midair as if uncertain what to do.

"You've never been a very conformable man, David," she agreed in a husky whisper. "You were pushy right from the start."

"So you think you'll get rid of me just by saying goodbye?"

"I don't know. Won't I?"

He shook his head. She wrapped her palm around his jaw. "I won't?"

"Do you want to? Get rid of me, I mean?"

And then a terrible thing happened. A mist of tears filled her beautiful green eyes.

And he couldn't help himself. He tugged her close and kissed her eyelids shut as a tear trickled down. She opened her eyes again.

"I'm sorry," she said with another gentle shake of her head. "I know this is a game we're playing, and I—I seem to have forgotten the rules."

"No rules. No game." His voice was a harsh, choked whisper. He thumbed away the dampness from her cheeks.

"It never was a game with us, really. Was it?" she asked.

He shook his head slowly, leaned forward and brushed her forehead with his lips. "I wanted it to be. I suspect we both wanted it to be, but no, it never was a game. What went on between us was as real as it gets, angel."

She pulled back, touched her fingertips to his lips, staring earnestly into his eyes. "I don't want to distress you, David. I promised I wouldn't be this way, but I don't want it to end. I don't want you to go."

"Try and make me leave you. I couldn't," he whispered against her fingertips, biting softly on the flesh.

The softest of smiles brightened her eyes. Her lips curved upward, giving him the response he needed and was desperate to have.

"I can give Rafe my notice," she offered.

"Too late. When I was in the Billings office, I saw that there was a position opening. It can be mine. I've grown to realize how much I love this place where I grew up. I thought about it on the ride back to White horn yesterday. I half considered applying for it, but—"

"You've changed your mind?" Confusion colored her expression.

"I've made up my mind," he confessed. "Gretchen, you've taught me a few things since I've been here. You've made me see that I've always pushed away the things I really wanted because I grew up knowing I couldn't have so many of my heart's desires. Denying those things has become a bad habit, a protective armor...

"You've changed things, though. I don't want to deny those wants and needs anymore, and what I really want is you. Day and night, in every way that counts. I know the thought of teaming up with any man permanently isn't your idea of heaven, but I'll do my best to make it work for you. I can't promise not to invade your space from time to time, but I'll try hard not to. I'm sure you'll remind me when you need time alone, and I'll do my best to protect you from people who ask too much from you. But I just can't imagine my world without you anymore, love. Do you think you could ever love me in the same way?"

Gretchen felt her heart filling up, her throat closing.

"Who gets to lead and who follows?" she asked with a teary smile.

He smiled back and she knew that look in his eyes was the love she wanted to see.

"We'll take turns," he promised.

She rose up on her toes and kissed him. Once. Twice. Too many times to count.

"I wonder if that will work," she whispered.

He slanted his lips over hers in one quick, hard, answering kiss. "You know that it will, lady. It's what we've been doing all along. Besides, you have to marry me now."

She grinned and looked down at her stomach. "I have to marry you? I'm not pregnant."

He chuckled and the sound thrilled her completely. "I hope you will be very soon. Besides, you have to marry me for one other reason, Gretchen. We've already planned our wedding."

She smiled up at him and watched his dark emerald eyes grow warm in that way that she knew she would always love. "I guess we have planned our wedding, but even if we hadn't, it wouldn't matter, David, my heart. I love you beyond belief. I'll marry you whenever you say."

"Today?"

"Or maybe yesterday," she agreed.

He grinned and pulled her in close for a kiss. "Your call this time," he said.

And she raised her lips to meet his. She claimed the man who owned her heart.

"Welcome to Whitehorn, love," she finally whispered. "I think this forever partnership is a wonderful idea."

And he folded her close and showed her just how very much in tune their thoughts were and would always be.

* * * * *

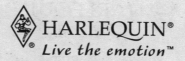

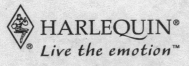

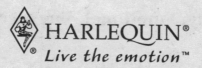

HARLEQUIN®

Super Romance®

...there's more to the story!

Superromance.
A *big* satisfying read about unforgettable characters. Each month we offer *six* very different stories that range from family drama to adventure and mystery, from highly emotional stories to romantic comedies—and much more! Stories about people you'll believe in and care about. Stories too compelling to put down....

Our authors are among today's *best* romance writers. You'll find familiar names and talented newcomers. Many of them are award winners—and you'll see why!

If you want the biggest and best in romance fiction, you'll get it from Superromance!

Exciting, Emotional, Unexpected...

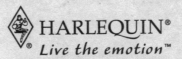

HARLEQUIN®
Live the emotion™

Harlequin® Historical
Historical Romantic Adventure!

Imagine a time of chivalrous knights and unconventional ladies, roguish rakes and impetuous heiresses, rugged cowboys and spirited frontierswomen—these rich and vivid tales will capture your imagination!

Harlequin Historical...
they're too good to miss!

HHDIR06

HEARTWARMING INSPIRATIONAL ROMANCE

Contemporary,
inspirational romances
with Christian characters
facing the challenges
of life and love
in today's world.

**NOW AVAILABLE IN REGULAR
AND LARGER-PRINT FORMATS.**

Steeple
Hill®

For exciting stories that reflect traditional values,
visit:
www.SteepleHill.com

Love Inspired® SUSPENSE

RIVETING INSPIRATIONAL ROMANCE

Watch for our new series of
edge-of-your-seat suspense novels.
These contemporary tales
of intrigue and romance
feature Christian characters
facing challenges to their faith...
and their lives!

Steeple
Hill®

Visit:
www.SteepleHill.com